ANDY'S SONG

Other books by Mary Leask:

Also set in Stewart's Falls:
Renovating Love
Two Cupids Too Many

ANDY'S SONG
•
Mary Leask

AVALON BOOKS
NEW YORK

PRINTED IN THE UNITED STATES OF AMERICA
ON ACID-FREE PAPER
BY HADDON CRAFTSMEN, BLOOMSBURG, PENNSYLVANIA

This book is dedicated to Mac and Heather;
to my writing buddies Karen, Sarah, Eleanor,
and Gillian; and to my patient writing
companions in Toronto.

It is also dedicated to Vera, whose home was
the inspiration for the house in this story.

Chapter One

Andrew Thompson brought his van to a stop in the parking lot of the Stewart's Falls Animal Clinic. Instead of getting out of his car immediately, he sat for a few moments to look at the scene before him.

Two tall firs framed a field of corn stubble, bleached as pale as cotton against the hard, brown earth. The grasses that edged the field were equally faded, matted together by melting snows and March winds. Small leafless shrubs, their darker branches penciled in against the seared background, trembled in the brisk breeze that blew dust and dried leaves across the parking lot and out over the field of cut-off corn stalks.

Andy shivered. The end of winter in southern Ontario was the pits. Zipping up his jacket, he hopped out of the van. The rush of cold wind had him pulling up his collar before he opened the van's side door and lifted out his tool box. Looping a coil of electrical wire over his arm, he closed the van and headed up the walk to the entrance of the clinic.

Just as he reached the steps, he happened to glance to his left. In the corner made by the steps and the building, where a shaft of sunlight warmed the walls, a cluster of crocuses glowed as bright as pirate's gold. He couldn't resist putting down his load and bending over to touch the tiny petals. Pushing away a few dried leaves, he discovered still more of the dainty buds and blooms: yellow, purple, and white.

As he picked up his tool box and cable and headed inside, a feeling of well-being curled up inside him, one that made him forget the blighted countryside and look forward to the rest of the day.

Andy passed through a short hall and paused at the doorway of the taupe-colored waiting room with its colorful animal posters and large aquarium. Several people waited. A small black and white dog shivered on the lap of Fred Timms, the owner of the restaurant on Main Street. Andy grinned. He knew faking when he saw it. He just bet that if Gina, the receptionist, were to drop a doggy treat in front of Rascal, it would be after it in a moment. The animal's eyes were far too bright, its ears too alert for real illness.

Several chairs away from Fred, George Collins held a cage on his lap containing Augustus, the biggest and orneriest cat in the village. It was making evil eyes at Fred's dog. No wonder Rascal shivered. *I would too*, thought Andy. He remembered doing some work at George's house. The cat's idea of fun was to lurk under a chair and wait until someone passed. Then, with its claws unsheathed, it would reach out and whack the innocent passerby. Andy had the scars to prove it.

The last client waiting was Roberto, the local hairdresser. He was the only man in the village besides Andy to let his hair grow long. There was a difference, though. While

Roberto's hair was a mass of unruly curls that drifted over his shoulder, Andy's was straight and smoothly caught at his nape with a clip. Andy knew that Roberto had a young, exuberant Lakeland Terrier named Dash. He wondered what mischief Dash had been up to.

Gina, the receptionist, sat behind the counter, her back turned away from the rest of the room as she talked on the telephone. He liked to tease Gina. She always responded with a gurgle of laughter that, for some reason, warmed his heart.

Then Andy had an idea. After all, it was April Fools' Day. Grinning, he tip-toed across the room. When he reached the counter, he waited until the moment Gina put down the telephone receiver then whispered, "Gina. You have a spider on your collar."

Gina went straight up in the air, half-turning to face him. "Take it off," she demanded.

"April Fools'." He laughed.

Laughing in spite of herself, Gina reached for him, but he stepped back. "Just you wait, Andy Thompson," she said. "Your day will come. Get out of here. Dr. Harper is waiting for you. Go through that door."

Andy met Mel, the technician, coming down the hall with Roberto's young Lakeland Terrier straining on the lead. Andy stopped to ruffle the dog's ears, saying, "Roberto's got a live one here."

"You're too right," replied Mel. "This character had to have stitches after his latest escapade."

As if he was anxious to show off his wound, the dog suddenly sat down and held up his paw with its bandage. Mel took a tidbit out of his pocket and gave it to the animal. "That's a good dog, Dash."

"He's a ham," Andy observed. "By the way, where do I find Dr. Harper?"

Mel pointed to the examining room to the right. "Just knock and go in. She's waiting for you."

Dr. Meredith Harper watched the good-looking electrician as he spread out the plans for the new equipment her partner, Dr. Dan Jameson, had ordered. Tall, broad-shouldered, and narrow-hipped, he should have been the most confident male in Stewart's Falls, but she knew that Andrew Thompson was considered shy. From the little she'd seen of him, she was more inclined to think that he was just reserved; soft-spoken and always polite but not nearly as out-going as his sister, Carolyn. She knew that he'd married his childhood sweetheart. Tragically, she had died from leukemia a number of years ago.

Merry understood how tragedy affected a person. Since the death of her husband two years earlier, she had found that she lived one day at a time, managing to deal with her job and her young son but not ready to deal with others on a deeply personal level. Moving to Stewart's Falls had been a good idea. Learning the ins and outs of the new practice kept her busy and helped ease her grief.

Andy straightened from the plans and asked, "Do you know where the power box is, Dr. Harper? Did Dan leave a plan of the building's wiring?"

Merry smiled. "Call me Merry. Everyone else does. The power box is in the cupboard at the end of the hall."

Folding up the plans, he said, "I'll call you Merry if you'll call me Andy. Will I be in your way while I'm checking out the wiring? I've got to figure the load on each line."

Merry thought for a moment. "The best thing to do is to

ask Gina if I have a patient. If I do, she can judge if it's alright to come in. Some animals are just fine with strangers. Others are frightened or distracted or just plain mean."

Andy grinned, and she was quite stunned by the difference this smile made. *He should do that more often*, she thought. *Half the women in Stewart's Falls would be after him.* He said, "You mean Augustus when you refer to meanness, I suspect."

She laughed. "I see his reputation goes before him. George seems to be the only person he'll tolerate. However, I've found his weakness. He's a sucker for a cat candy."

"I wish I'd known that when he attacked my ankle," Andy said. "I very nearly charged George danger pay when I did some work for him."

Laughing, they both left the room where they met Mel coming out of another examining room. "Augustus is waiting for you, Merry. Better get some armor."

She took a package of cat tidbits out of her pocket and waved them in front of Mel. "I've got all the armor I need right here." Turning to Andy, she added, "As technician, Mel probably knows more about the wiring in this place than I do. Mel, would you see if you can answer Andy's questions? I'll be free after I see Augustus and Rascal."

Mel groaned. "Oh, Merry, I'm sorry. I forgot. Dan left me a plan of the wiring. I'll get it for Andy."

She watched for a moment as the tall electrician followed Mel into Dan's office to get the plan. *That man's blue eyes are enough to win any woman's heart*, she thought. *Wonder if Gina's noticed them.* Then, giving the package another shake, she opened the door, ready to see what Augustus's problem was today.

* * *

Gina closed the waiting room door and hung up the 'Gone to Lunch' sign. While headed down the hall to the library, which doubled as a lunch room, she met Andy. "If you have your lunch, bring it in and eat it with us." Pointing to the library door, she said, "We meet in there."

As she entered the library she thought that it was too bad they had agreed that April Fools jokes should end at noon. She'd have been tempted to put something in his lunch.

Gina listened quietly as the rest of the staff and Andy chatted as they ate their lunch. Remembering that Augustus had been in, she asked, "How'd it go with George's cat, Merry?"

Merry held up her hands. "See. No scratches."

Mel shook his head. "You're a miracle worker. The one time I tangled with that cat, he bit my thumb. Hurt like crazy. Even Doctor Dan's had a scratch or two. Speaking of Dan, I wonder where the honeymooners are now. Does anyone know?"

"Are you kidding?" Merry asked, grinning. "Dan kept travel folders locked in his desk. He always seemed to be making mysterious phone calls. Kept hanging up when anyone came near." Looking across at Gina, Merry continued. "I suppose if anyone would have a clue, it would be you, Gina. Know anything?"

Gina held up her hands. "My lips are sealed."

Jane, the second technician piped up. "You were at the wedding, Gina. What was it like?"

"It was very nice," she replied. "Cindy wore a lovely ivory gown trimmed in lace. Her veil was caught in a circle of rosebuds that nested in her hair. And . . . you could have lit the church with Dan's smile."

Turning to Andy, Gina said, "Your sister, Carolyn, looked lovely too. She wore a long blue gown just the color of her eyes."

Changing the subject, Andy asked Merry, "How's your little boy adjusting to Stewart's Falls. You've been here about four months now. Has he made any friends?"

"Ruth, my nanny-cum-housekeeper lives in and has a little boy almost the same age. They have a good time together." She paused for a second, then said, "I remember now. You held Michael up so he could see the Santa Claus parade, didn't you?"

Andy nodded. He'd been quite enchanted with the little boy, all freckles, blue eyes and red hair. There had been something about the way the boy had perched on his shoulders so trustingly, his small arms about his neck that had made him suddenly wish for a boy of his own.

Packing up her lunch and standing up, Merry said, "Well, I'd better get to work. I want to leave early tonight." Turning to Gina, she said, "I'm off to see one of Jake Armstrong's horses. I'll be back in time for my three o'clock appointment."

Gina locked the door behind the last patient and its master and returned to her desk. Efficiently, she made a last entry into the computer and then tidied the desk area. Sitting back, she looked over her small kingdom with satisfaction. She loved her job. She felt so lucky to have it.

Taking out a folder, she began working on some material for Dr. Dan's new wife, Cindy.

Andy finished off his work for the day, packed up his equipment, and stored it where Mel had suggested. Closing his toolbox, he headed toward the waiting room. He was surprised to see that Gina was still there. She was watching something coming out of the printer and hadn't heard him.

Going over to the reception counter, Andy said, "Gina. Thought you'd be gone by now."

She jumped in the air at the sound of his voice. Turning toward him, her hand against her chest, she said, "You scared the wits out of me. I thought you'd already left."

"No, just finished. What's keeping you late?"

By now, the printer had stopped, and she took out a sheet of paper to show him. "As you know, Cindy hopes to open a new tearoom in late May. I'm making some sample set-ups for the menus Cindy will be using. This is my first attempt. I'm trying it with a number of different fonts and page set-ups. I thought I could save Cindy some time by putting together a few options for her."

Andy took the sheet from her and studied it. It looked pretty good to him, but then again, what did he know? Glancing up, he was surprised to see that Gina was watching from eyes that he'd never realized were a smoky mixture of brown and black. Eyes that were framed with the longest darn lashes he'd ever seen.

"What do you think?" she asked.

Pulling his attention back to the proffered paper, he said, "It looks clear and precise to me. But maybe she would like the lettering just a little fancier. Did she give you any suggestions?"

"No. I just thought I'd experiment. I think it will save Cindy time if I have some suggestions ready. After all, they want to open soon."

Looking at his watch, Andy said, "Well, it looks like it's

time to quit. It'll be dark soon." Glancing out the window, he frowned. "I don't see any car. How did you get here?"

"Usually, Mel takes me. Today, I wanted to stay to work on the menus. I'll walk home. It's not that far."

Not liking the idea of her walking alone, Andy said, "I'll be glad to give you a lift. I'll wait until you're ready."

"Thanks. I'll just go and get my coat."

Andy was intrigued as he watched her head into the nether regions of the clinic. He liked the way she walked; so full of energy and purpose for one so petite. In fact, he was beginning to realize that he liked a lot of things about her.

Gina's complexion mirrored her Italian background. At least, he thought it was Italian. Her surname was Falconi, and the way that her shiny dark hair curled tightly around her head and small, dainty face, gave him reason to believe that his theory was correct. How, Andy wondered, had the single young men of Stewart's Falls missed this gem?

As Andy walked with Gina out to the car, he couldn't help but notice that she only reached up to his shoulder. Andy moved to the passenger door of his van and unlocked it. He was just about to go around to his door when he noticed Gina eyeing the high step.

"Can I give you a hand up?" he asked. "You'll never make it up on to this seat with that long skirt on."

When she nodded, he assisted her into the high seat. As he did so, he caught a whiff of her shampoo. It reminded him of flowers and herbs.

Whistling away to himself, he walked around to his side of the van and swung easily into the seat. Starting the van, he asked, "Where exactly do you live?"

"Over on Elm Street. About four houses from the lake."

Andy knew the street. The house was one of the older houses in the village, probably built in the 1880s for the men and their families working at the long-gone lumber mill.

They drove in comfortable silence into the center of town and turned toward the lake. Andy had always loved this street. At one end, there was a Victorian mansion worthy of any early mill owner. At the other end were much smaller houses, each with a single Gothic window looking out of the second floor. He wondered which one Gina lived in.

She pointed out the house. Number 73. "It's the house with the little pine in front of it."

Gina lived in this house? It was the only house on the street that had not been renovated recently. The paint was peeling on the verandah and on the small display of ginger-bread trim.

Curious, he asked, "How long have you lived here, Gina?"

"Only for a year and a half. Before that, I lived with my grandmother in Toronto. When she died, she left this house to me. I didn't even know she owned it. It seems she had an elderly cousin living in it for years. Neither my grandmother or her cousin did much to keep it up to date. The only thing I can say for it is that it has plumbing, electricity, and great potential."

Turning to Andy, Gina said, "Thanks for the ride." Then, with an impish grin, she said, "Don't think for a moment that I've forgotten that spider trick. My moment will come. Live in suspense."

As she left the van and headed up the sidewalk, Andy wondered about the state of the house inside.

*   *   *

Andy headed home to the big gabled house that he shared with his father. When Carolyn had married and his younger brother Ben moved out, he had felt it necessary to move back to the family home to stay with his widowed father who had had heart surgery only months before. Even though his dad's recovery seemed miraculous, Andy had been uneasy about him staying alone.

Anyway, he thought ruefully, *it has been for the best.* He hadn't realized that his grief over the loss of his wife, Kelly, had isolated him from everyone. Carolyn's often humorous romance with David, and Ben's engagement to his nurse fiancée, Barbara, had made him realize what a recluse he had become. One lonely winter night, he'd decided that no one had control over the past, but one could shape one's future. He'd been deliberately trying to do this ever since.

His father was taking a casserole out of the oven just as Andy entered the kitchen. "Mmm," he said. "Something smells delicious."

"Nora says it's called *Cog au Vin*. I'm sure it will be delicious as usual."

"Where is Nora tonight?"

Nora was the housekeeper. She was there through the day and, as a rule, had supper with them; then she usually hurried off to her own small house to pursue her own interests.

The entire family had been relieved when they'd found Nora. Everyone worked long hours and had found it hard to help their father through his early convalescence. Fortunately, Nora and his dad got on well. Andy was sure her presence had contributed to his amazing recovery. Lately, they'd taken to playing bridge together at the nearby seniors' club.

Mary Leask

"Nora's at the historical society tonight. How's your day been?"

As the two of them sat down to enjoy Nora's excellent casserole, Andy described the wiring job he'd begun at the veterinarian clinic.

"Any interesting animal problems while you were there?"

Andy laughed. "Just Augustus, that fiendish cat of George Collins that dug his claws into me."

His father grinned. "I don't know why someone hasn't spirited that cat away when George wasn't looking. He's a menace."

After a few more mouthfuls, his father asked, "How's the new vet doing while Dan is on his honeymoon?"

"You mean Dr. Harper?"

His dad nodded.

"She seems to be doing fine, although this is just the third day she's been on her own. I'm sure she knows what she's doing."

"How's her little boy getting along?"

"I asked her that today. She says he's adjusting quite well, especially since Ruth Dodd and her little boy are living with them."

Suddenly, Andy remembered the house he'd delivered Gina to. "You know those story-and-a-half houses over on Elm Street?"

His father nodded.

"Well, I took the receptionist, Gina, home from work today. She's living in the fourth house from the lake."

His father's eyebrows lifted at that news. "That's the one old Miss Davidson lived in for years. I was in there once to wire a washer and dryer. I sure hope some work has been done on it since then. It was in terrible shape. I used to wonder how she stayed warm in the winter. I'm sure it wasn't insulated properly."

"I'm sure you're right," said Andy. "I've been in some of them too. The walls are just stuffed with anything they could find to cut down the cold."

His father nodded in agreement. "I think it was a miracle that they didn't all burn down. There would have had to be very hot fires to keep them liveable."

"Well," said Andy, "I sure hope it's been renovated for Gina's sake."

When supper was finished, Andy helped his father clean up and then headed upstairs. Taking out a guitar, his companion for the past dark years, he sat down and warmed up, running his fingers lovingly over the strings, trying chord after chord until his mind was firmly in a world of sound. But tonight, it was not enough. Tonight, he wanted something livelier. Words seemed to hop right into his head.

"Yellow bird sat on an orange cat's head."

Where on earth had that idea come from? But he liked it. It was the kind of song you could sing to young children. The image of Merry's little boy came to him. Would he laugh at such an idea? Andy thought for a few moments, unconsciously trying rhythms and tunes as he concentrated on the words.

" 'What's on my head?' the orange cat said."

For the rest of the evening, he amused himself, trying out lines and tunes.

* * *

Gina hurriedly shut the door of the house and watched Andy start the van and move up the street. What if he had walked her up to the door? Andy was just the kind of guy that would do something like that. What if she'd felt obliged to ask him in for a coffee? She shuddered at the thought as she hurried through the small hall and into the main room, heading over to the big, old-fashioned range that took up a good portion of the room. For sure, Andy would have noticed the cold. Peeking into the firebox, she was relieved to see that the coals were still red. Quickly, she added some logs and adjusted the draft. In a half an hour, the house would be as warm as toast.

She had been lucky that Dan, her boss, had never walked her to the door when they were dating. But of course he hadn't; their relationship had always been a platonic one. All along, Dan's true love had been Cindy, and Gina had so nearly messed up that romance by misleading Cindy. She thanked the heavens that Dan and Cindy had forgiven her.

Hurriedly, she hung up her jacket and scarf in the tiny entrance and went into the equally small and antiquated bathroom. Here, a tiny electrical heater installed in the wall kept the water in the pipes warm. Stepping out of her long denim skirt and removing the sweater she wore at the office, she pulled on a set of ski underwear. Over that, she pulled on a -t-shirt, a plaid shirt, and heavy jeans. Sitting on the side of the shoddy little tub, she pulled on socks and stepped into warm moccasins. Checking herself in the mirror, she was amused in spite of herself. She looked like a heroine in a pioneer romance.

There were only four working appliances in the house: the refrigerator, a washer and dryer her grandmother's cousin must have picked up second hand, and an ancient microwave. Going to the fridge, she took out a frozen container of chili she'd made on the weekend. *Thank goodness for the microwave*, she thought. She was starving. If she'd had to use the wood stove, it would have taken forever.

As Gina ate, she examined her surroundings. It probably would have been alright to bring Andy in. She had already done some redecorating. The room she sat in must have always been the most important in the house. At some time, an owner had put in new kitchen cupboards, which included a counter with a sink. An extra room had been added that opened off this main area. Right now, Gina used it for a bedroom, but originally it must have been used as a dining room or family room.

At the front of the house, there were two more rooms. One had obviously been the parlor, while the one beside it had been a bedroom. Each room had interesting old furniture, and Gina was sure that when she could afford to have the house rewired and proper heating installed, she would refinish the old pieces and make two very pleasant rooms.

Up the narrow stairs were two bedrooms. For now, the second floor and the two rooms in the front were shut off.

Finishing her meal, Gina took her dishes and cutlery over to the sink and washed up. She was quite happy with the work she'd done in the kitchen. She'd painted the dark cupboards a soft, traditional blue and then lightened the paint by rubbing in a white wash. She'd even managed to tile the back of the counter in white tiles. To add some color, she'd been fortunate enough to find a few painted tiles to lessen the impact of the white.

She'd painted an antique blue wainscoting on the old wallpaper and topped it with a matching tiny print pattern that picked up the blue and the colors in the tile. She'd also decorated the hallway to match the kitchen. Fortunately, the floor was made of pine planks that were worn but serviceable. At some point, she would have it properly refinished.

Really, she thought, *I don't have any reason to be ashamed of this section of the house*. Even though the bathroom had yet to be tackled, it was adequate. Maybe she was ready to have company.

Satisfied that the room was tidy, Gina went out into the tiny work shed behind the house. For some reason, this shed was wired separately, and she was able to turn on an electric heater. When she had tried the same heater in the house, the fuse had blown.

In the center of the shed, a three-drawer dresser she'd taken from the front rooms stood on a sheet of plastic. The drawers stood on another sheet of plastic. Gina had already stripped off the layers of paint that had been applied over the years. Underneath, she found the wood to be bird's eye maple. Once she had it sanded smooth, she intended to wax it. The knobs were original and she intended to put them back on. Taking up a sanding block, she set to work.

Merry sat in a comfortable arm chair before the fire working on a piece of tapestry. She found the meticulous needlework relaxing; it was a far cry from smelly barns, obstreperous cattle, and kicking horses. Tucked in beside her was Sweet Pea, the charming calico cat her son adored. Occasionally, the cat would bat a thread tentatively with her paw but only gently. She'd learned quite quickly that to do more was to be put away from the chair and the comfort of Merry's company.

Merry paused in her work for a moment, her most immediate problem intruding, breaking her concentration. It was the first of April now, and she only had until the first of June to find a permanent place to live.

She'd been very lucky to be able to rent Cindy's parents' home while they had been away in Florida and now in England. She'd only had to leave the house during the week of the wedding, and that had been no problem. She and her son had just moved over to a bed and breakfast during that time. But this home had been a nice change for Ruth and the boys as well as for her.

Tomorrow, she'd ask if anyone could recommend a good real estate agent. If she wasn't so content sitting before the fire, she could probably do some exploring on the Internet herself.

Still musing over the problem as she chose another color, she suddenly thought of Andy. It amazed her that that handsome, blue-eyed man was still unattached. A sudden urge to play Cupid had her thinking of Gina. Her happy personality was just what Andy needed. Now, if she could just get Andy interested in Gina.

Merry worked for a few minutes on a tricky section of her tapestry, and then her thoughts returned to Gina. It was hard to imagine the clinic without her. She welcomed the clients, entertained their pets, and certainly kept the business end of the practice up to date.

With a shake of her head, Merry returned to her main problem. Finding a home. She'd ask Andy if he knew of any. After all, he must know most of the homes in the village as he had probably worked on many of them.

Chapter Two

Andy worked all morning at the clinic. Because Merry had three surgeries booked, he spent his time up in the attic of the building, running lines to the room that would hold the new equipment. By noon, he was hungry and tired of working behind a mask designed to protect him against the insulation.

After freshening up, Andy realized that he'd left his lunch in the car. When he stepped outside, he noticed an older black pickup with a crooked license plate rattle out of the driveway and disappear down the road toward town. It wasn't a truck he recognized. *Must have been lost and turned around*, he thought. As he hurried to his van, he realized that the air was warmer. He stopped for a moment and breathed in its softness. It smelled like spring. The lilt of a tune teased his imagination, but he was unable to capture it.

He got his lunch and headed back to the clinic. Just as he was about to climb the steps, he glanced down at the crocuses. He was annoyed to discover that a small cardboard box had been plunked down right on top of the flowers.

Even as he stooped to lift the box off the fragile flowers, it moved. It was then that he realized that the box had crudely cut small holes along the side. Lifting the box off the crocuses, he was pleased to see the yellow blooms spring back up.

His attention was drawn back to the box when whatever was inside shifted, and he heard a faint scrabbling and a noise that sounded suspiciously like a high-pitched mew. Grinning to himself, Andy thought, *wait until the others see what I've found for lunch.*

Everyone was eating when Andy entered the lunch room. With a flourish, Andy placed the box in the center of the table and said, "Here's a special lunch treat someone left beside your front steps."

Gina was the first to respond. Quickly, she tore off the electrical tape that held the box closed and opened the flaps. The rest joined her in peeking into the box. There they discovered three very small kittens, hardly old enough to totter about, their ears barely erect, their little tails standing up like small spikes.

"Oh," breathed Gina. "Aren't they adorable." She reached in and picked up a tiny orange tabby and placed it on the table. The small creature cried plaintively and staggered forward, obviously searching for its mother. Unable to resist, Gina picked it up and cuddled it against her face. "Oh, the poor wee thing," she crooned.

Merry, equally enthralled, picked up a tiny, grey-striped Persian that kept trying to nibble on her finger. Andy couldn't resist the third little fellow, as black as night with just a spot of white under his chin and on the tip of his tail. He cradled it in his hand and the small creature purred.

"They're starving," Merry said briskly. Handing the kitten over to Mel, she said, "I'll make some mash from kitten kibble. I think they're old enough to manage that."

For the rest of the lunch hour, they took turns trying to get the kittens to eat. There was a great deal of laughter as Andy's black kitten shoved his face in the food and then sneezed, frightening the kitten and leaving an endearing spatter of food on his whiskers. When the kittens had had enough, and their faces had been cleaned with a damp tissue, they stumbled around the lunch table checking out lunch bags and swatting bits of paper. Then, like all young things that have just been fed, they began to yawn. Gina gently placed them in her lap, where they snuggled together and slept.

"Where do you think they came from?" asked Gina.

"When I went out to get my lunch," Andy said, "there was a black pickup just disappearing out of the lane. I thought it must have been someone turning around. Maybe whoever was driving left the kittens."

"You know," said Merry, "I would guess that someone found the kittens without a mother and, rather than leave them to starve in the cold, took them to the only place they might be cared for."

"But you know, Merry," said Mel glumly, "We don't make a practice of taking in every lost animal. We'd have no room for the ones who are sick if we did."

"I know," said Merry.

"Do you think I could have them?" asked Gina.

"They'll take a lot of attention over the next week or so until they're weaned," Merry warned. "You might have to do some hand-feeding. You will definitely have to keep them clean. How do you feel about feeding them several times a night?"

Gina touched the tiny heads gently. "I'd love to care for them."

"Great," Merry said, "We can help you with food and shots. And when it comes time for neutering, I expect Dan and I could find it in our hearts to do it for you."

Absolutely beaming, Gina placed the kittens in the box and headed toward the hall. "I'll need to get them something better to sleep in."

The two technicians stood together. "I'll find a cage for you," said Jane. "C'mon, Mel. Let's give Gina a hand."

Andy and Merry watched in silence as the three of them rushed out. "Well, I'm glad we've found a home for the kittens," Merry said. "We can count on Gina doing a good job."

Merry began to pack up her lunch then paused and said to Andy, "Oh, by the way, I have an electrical problem and I wondered if you could check it out for me. There's no great rush. Just whenever you can fit it in."

"What's the problem?" he asked.

"When I use the hair dryer in the bathroom, the ground fault switch snaps off. But, you don't need to fix it immediately; I can manage with damp hair now that it's getting warmer out. I wonder if you could come either some day after work or maybe on a Saturday. I guess it depends on both our schedules."

"I can't do it tonight 'cause I've already got an appointment. How about tomorrow night, say seven-thirty?"

"That sounds perfect. You know where I live?"

Andy nodded. "I've done work for Cindy's family before. I just hope it isn't something I've done that's gone wrong. Anyway, we'll check it out."

* * *

That afternoon, after Andy had put his tools away, he headed into the reception room. There was still one patient, a portly pig, sitting like a dog beside his master. Andy waved at the gentleman holding the pig's leash. "Hope Leander is alright, Howard."

Howard smiled. "Just his usual yearly check up. I think he may have gained just a little too much weight."

Andy caught Gina's eye at this, and it was all either of them could do not to laugh. Leander had drooping jowls and a pot-belly that declared his love for food.

Andy went over to check on Gina's new family. All three kittens were piled together sound asleep in a corner of the cage that had been found for them. At one end of the cage sat a box of litter. Pointing at it, Gina said proudly, "They know how to use the litter. I've had to clean it out already."

Andy said, "I'll take you and your brood home when you're ready to go. It's just around the corner from where I live."

Gina positively glowed. "Would you? Mel is having trouble with his car. He rode his bike this morning. I thought I'd have to take a taxi home. I shouldn't be more than another half hour."

"Good. I've still got a few things I can do to get ready for tomorrow." *And*, Andy thought to himself, *I can make sure I get into Gina's house and check to see that it's safe.*

As Andy pulled up in front of Gina's place, he took a better look at the house he had driven past for years, dismissing it for its shabby exterior. It was a classic example of a story-and-a-half. If he remembered his architectural history, these houses were built with the half-story to avoid paying taxes for two floors.

Across the front was a verandah supported by four square columns. Above the verandah was the traditional peaked gable with its pointed Gothic window. Under the verandah roof, he could see that the main entrance was flanked by two windows. With some good hard work, it could be a beautiful house. It was just crying out for some tender, loving care.

Andy followed Gina to a side door near the back of the house and was surprised when he entered the small hall. It was nicely papered and painted in a traditional style suiting the house's age. "Who did the decorating?" he asked.

"I did."

"Well, you chose very well. I feel like I've stepped into the nineteenth century."

Gina's face flushed with pleasure at his praise. "Thanks."

"Where shall I put the kittens?"

Leading him into the main room, she pointed, "I think the best place would be beside the stove."

As he set down the kittens, he became aware of something else. The room was cold. It felt about fifty-five degrees. Andy tried to hide a shiver.

Gina was already lifting the rounded lid on the firebox to check on the embers. "I'll just put some logs in here, and the place will warm up in no time."

Andy was concerned now. "Is the stove your only source of heat, Gina?"

"There are some electric wall heaters, but one of them sparked so I'm afraid to use them."

To Gina's dismay, Andy began to walk around the kitchen and the living room-cum-bedroom, checking outlets and heaters. Then he went out into the hall and the bathroom.

Gina didn't know whether to be annoyed or amused at the

single-minded way in which Andy investigated her wiring. When he came out of the bathroom he said, "There's an in-wall heater in there. Does it work?"

Gina nodded. "I think it's wired separately. So is the work shed at the back."

"You need to have this house rewired."

Suddenly, Gina was angry. "I would think that's obvious to anyone, Andy. But it costs money. Until I have enough, I'll make do with my old stove and microwave."

Andy smiled and Gina felt its impact right down to her toes. *He should smile like that every day*, she thought.

"I'm sorry," he said. "*I'm* sounding like an officious idiot. How come you're living in this house? Surely you could rent an apartment that would be safer and warmer."

"Like I told you, I inherited the house from my grand-mother. She brought me up and when she died two years ago, she left this house to me."

Gina went over to a small desk that held her telephone. Above it was a portrait of an elderly woman. Pointing to her, Gina said softly, "This is my grandmother, taken about six years ago. She left a letter for me with her will. She said I needed a home of my own. She hoped that in time, I'd be able to live here and fix it up. She left a little money, and I'm saving for enough to get the house rewired and new wall heaters installed. Then I can start fixing up the rest of the house. It's cheaper to live here than pay rent. It means I can save money faster."

"Don't you have any other family, Gina?"

"I have a much older step-sister. My mother married twice. I'm the product of her second marriage. My grand-mother took me in when my parents were killed in an accident. At that point, my step-sister was in college and in no position to take in a ten-year-old."

"You must miss your grandmother very much."

Gina was touched that he'd understand that. "I do. That's why I'm so determined to make a go of this house. It was her dream for me."

Andy glanced at his watch. "I've got to go. What are you going to do with the kittens while you're at work?"

"I've decided to take them with me. Merry thinks our clients will be interested in watching them. Also, some client might just decide they would like a kitten."

"How do you intend to get them back and forth from work?"

"Mel said he'd pick me up once his car is fixed. I'm going to watch out for a second-hand bicycle. I think the snow is finished. I'm sure I could fix a box on it to take the kittens back and forth. However, I'm not sure what I'll do tomorrow morning."

"I'll pick you up."

She gave him a delightful smile. "Thank you. I'd appreciate that."

As he drove over to his father's house, Andy thought about Gina. There was a lot more to her than he had initially realized. It took courage to take on that old house single-handed. And so far, she seemed to have made sensible decisions.

Andy's appointment that night was at the library. Once a week for eight weeks he attended a class on computers. It was time he caught up with the rest of the family.

When he stepped into the charming, limestone library, he had to figure out just where to go. The building was a warren of rooms; one even had a fireplace. Margaret Henshaw, the librarian, hurried from one of the rooms. When she saw him, she said, "Hi, Andy. Are you here for the computer class, the upgrading program, or to get a book?"

"The computer class."

She pointed, "It's just down that small hall. The room on your right." With that, she bustled over to the student volunteer behind the check-out desk. "Everything under control?"

Andy saw the girl nod and then watched as the librarian rushed into one of the other rooms as he headed for the computer class.

There was a bank of eight computers along one wall. Seven of them already had a person in front of them. He headed for the eighth. Settling himself down before the machine, he turned to the person beside him. It was George, Augustus's master.

Andy couldn't help teasing, "I see you managed to escape Augustus tonight, George."

"He's at home, happily crunching on some treats. He sleeps most of the time anyway. He's not as young as he looks."

In a low voice, Andy asked, "Do you know anything about computers, George?"

George looked as sheepish as Andy felt. "I couldn't turn one on if my life depended on it. The cat probably knows more than I do."

"I'm just the same. Don't need them at work. I can still use my pen. However, I know Carolyn. She'll soon be sending me out on jobs with the description in one of those palm things."

George nodded. "I know what you mean. I'm an upholsterer. You don't need a computer for that. But my assistant is always nagging that we need a computer so that he can get information on the Internet about fabric and patterns. He says that I could learn to do the ordering and accounting too. Decided I'd better learn if I wanted to stay in charge of my own business."

"Must be fun working on chairs with Augustus around."

George smiled. "It's easier now. Once, when he was a kitten, he climbed into the interior of a sofa just before I was closing it up. Well, he must have fallen asleep in there, because later, when I couldn't find him, I called his name and start hearing this pitiful crying coming from the workroom. It took me ages to figure out where the sound was coming from. He's a lot more careful these days."

George looked back at the computer and gingerly ran his fingers over the keyboard. "You know, I never learned to type. My assistant says it doesn't matter. He says one can hunt and peck if necessary."

Andy was just about to say he'd taken typing in high school when he heard a familiar voice say, "Good evening, class. I'm your teacher, Gina Falconi."

Andy froze at the sound of those words. Were the fates punishing him for teasing Gina? How was he going to keep his cool with this beast of a machine facing him? He hated the thought of making a fool of himself in front of her. Taking a calming breath, he turned around and said, "Hi, Gina."

He realized immediately that she was nervous. Her cheeks flushed and her fingers trembled slightly as she set down some papers. "Hi, Andy. Didn't realize you'd be in this ___." Turning to the other students, she said, "I'll just get ___ your names down on this sheet for me."

___ was passed around, Andy kept an eye on ___ looking casually smart this evening. She wore a soft pink turtleneck sweater and black pants, topped by a black jacket. She even had shoes with heels on. *Very much the little teacher*, he thought with amusement and then remembered that if anyone was going to be amused that evening, it would be Gina. Just wait 'til she saw him try to fumble with the keyboard. It was so long since he'd touched a typewriter, that he'd probably be worse than George.

Gina handed out a set of papers to each student. Andy eyed them suspiciously.

She must have sensed the ripple of unease from her students because she said, "Just tuck those papers along the side of the computer for now. I just want you to become familiar with the computer first before we do any exercises."

She handed them labels and felt tip pens. "For my sake, print your name on the label and stick it on the edge of the machine so I can get to know who you are."

She waited as they all industriously penned their names on the labels and placed them where they could be seen. "Now," she said, pointing at the monitor, "who knows what you call this?"

Most of the hands went up. She asked a middle-aged woman, "Yes, Marion?"

"I believe it's called the monitor."

"Absolutely right," said Gina.

And that's how she proceeded. Asking questions that allowed her students to show off the little knowledge they had. Soon, they were relaxed enough that she had them turn on their computers. "Usually they'll be on, but I thought it was important that you understand how to turn them off and on. I remember when I first encountered a computer. The teacher made all kinds of assumptions. It made me feel really stupid."

Andy felt himself relax as she directed them how to use the programs, bring down windows, and open, close, delete, and save files.

Finally, she directed them to look at the first of the papers she had given them. "There are some easy directions I want you to follow. If you get in trouble, just ask. You can always ask each other, also. Just talk quietly so everyone else can still concentrate."

For a few moments, everyone worked in silence. Then, Andy heard George mutter, "Darn mouse. Won't do anything I want."

Immediately, Gina was leaning over between them, saying, "Let me try your mouse, George. Sometimes, they need cleaning."

As Gina fiddled with the mouse, Andy was again aware of the fragrance she wore; that subtle mixture of flowers and herbs. It reminded him of a spring meadow. He wondered if George found it lovely. He glanced over at his partner only to find him smiling at Gina as he steered his mouse across the screen. *She's a good teacher*, thought Andy.

As the class ended, Andy suddenly became aware that it was raining outside. Turning toward Gina, he was just in time to hear George say, "Do you need a ride home, Gina? I can go right past your house."

It was all Andy could do to keep from scowling when he heard her say, "Thanks, George. I'd really appreciate a ride." Looking down at her shoes, she said ruefully, "I didn't check the weather report before I came out. I don't want to ruin my shoes."

Feeling somewhat disgruntled, Andy packed up his notes and left.

* * *

When Andy returned home that night, he found his father playing Cribbage with Nora. They finished just as he headed to the kitchen to raid the fridge. Andy was starving, because he had been late for dinner and had hardly had time to do justice to Nora's roast beef. As he sliced beef off the roast, his father called in to him, "I'm just going to walk Nora home. If you're making tea, save a cup for me."

Andy had been going to make coffee, but if his father felt like tea, so be it. It would have to be decaffeinated. *Oh well*, Andy thought, *probably better for me anyway.*

Five minutes later, Andy's father, Jim Thompson, returned and settled down at the kitchen table with a cup of tea and a cookie. "How was the computer class?" he inquired.

Andy grimaced. "I know how kids feel when they start grade one. There is so much to take in. So much to remember."

Jim nodded in agreement. "I remember when Carolyn insisted we needed to have a computer for the business. I thought I'd never get the hang of it. After a while, though, all that information settles in and it seems quite simple."

"I hope so."

"How was the teacher?"

"Now, that was a surprise. Gina Falconi is the teacher. And a good one, too. She admitted after class that it was her first session. I thought she did very well. She certainly was patient with all of us."

They both sipped their tea in silence for a few minutes and then Andy remembered his day.

"You'll never guess what happened at work."

"George's cat had kittens," quipped Jim.

"No, but you're close. When I went out to get my lunch, I

found a box containing three kittens. They were hardly old enough to leave their mother. Cute little devils."

"What on earth will they do with them at the clinic?"

"Gina has decided to look after them. She's going to take them home each evening until they're able to get through a night without a feeding. They're hoping a client will be so taken with them that they'll offer to give them a home."

Jim smiled in recollection. "Do you remember those kittens Carolyn found half-starved? When I told her we couldn't possibly look after them, Carolyn was broken-hearted. Your mother finally convinced me that Carolyn could keep them on the condition that she got up at night to feed them."

Andy grinned. "I remember. Mike, Ben and I, being the older brothers, did most of the getting up. It was just as hard when the kittens were old enough to give away. By then, we were all foster parents."

"And Lucy lived to be sixteen. I still miss her sometimes."

Andy laughed. "I'm sure we have just the cat for you. Would you like black, orange, or tabby?"

"Not a chance," Jim declared.

Then Andy remembered Gina's house. "I checked over the rooms Gina's using in that house. Not only is the wiring ancient, but the electric heaters are sparking."

Alarmed, Jim said, "You mean she's using those heaters?"

"No. She's been quite sensible. She's using that old stove for heat, and I gather she probably cooks on it too, though she's got a microwave. She's trying to save enough to have the place rewired."

Jim thought for a moment. "You know, I think I read of a

government-funded program offering assistance to people trying to update their electrical systems in century homes. There have been too many fires in the past. I think the program is looking to fix that. I'll see if I can track it down. Probably pretty easy to do on the Internet."

Andy pulled a face. Even his father was a new age guy. That's what came of living like a hermit and feeling sorry for himself. Then he remembered another idea he'd had.

"Is Carolyn's old bike still in the basement?"

"I think so."

"Do you think she'd mind if I gave it to Gina? She has no means of transportation. I thought I could fix up a box to fit over the back bumper. She could take the kittens back and forth to work until they're a little more independent."

Jim brightened at that idea. "I'll look after it. I think I have the material in the garage to make a box for it. I'm sure Carolyn has forgotten she ever had the bike, let alone that it's still in the basement."

Very pleased with that, Andy stood, put his dishes in the dishwasher, and headed out of the kitchen. Just at the door, he paused, "Oh, by the way. I'm going to Dr. Harper's tomorrow night to repair a ground fault switch in the bathroom. Did we put that in?"

"I did, but it was about ten years ago. Those units do wear out."

Jim watched his son disappear down the hall. A tightness around his heart that he'd never known was there seemed to lighten. For the first time in years, the light was back in Andy's eyes. Something good seemed to be happening. He wondered what it was.

* * *

Gina sat on the rocking chair in front of the old stove watching the kittens' antics. They were always active just before her bedtime and tonight was no different. She was impressed how quickly they had adapted to their environment.

She'd found some old boards in the shed and created a small play area for them. In it, she put bits of paper, a tiny ball, and a little paper bag along with an old cardboard shoe box. Moment by moment, the kittens seemed to grow steadier on their feet. They tried to race at the balls of paper but their legs were uncoordinated, and their tiny rear ends often raced ahead. The black one had actually managed to discover the hole in the side of the shoe box and was busily trying to get his paw in to capture an imaginary mouse. She found herself laughing at his antics.

Finally, they seemed to lag, and she lifted them carefully on her lap where they settled in a warm, breathing clump of fur. She rocked gently and stroked their tiny bodies while she reviewed her evening.

She'd nearly had a fit when Andy Thompson had shown up for her class. His name hadn't been on her list, although she had been warned that there was a full class.

It was the first time she'd ever taught a computer class; something she had never thought of doing before. When the teacher originally hired for the job had become suddenly ill, the librarian had thought of Gina. When Gina realized that she would actually be paid for her time, she had taken the job to earn money for the wiring Andy had said was so necessary. Fortunately, the sick teacher had left a series of lesson plans, so all she had to do was follow the suggestions.

Smiling with a sense of real accomplishment, Gina realized that the night had been quite wonderful. She knew after a few moments that her students were just as nervous as she. It had given her a very warm feeling to be able to introduce them to the computer.

Chapter Three

Gina was surprised when Andy arrived earlier than she expected. "I've come to take you to the clinic. Then, I've got to work on an emergency problem in a house that Carolyn's renovating." While Gina rushed around, tidying away her breakfast, hastily brushing her hair, and adding some lipstick, Andy carried the kittens out to the car.

As they drove toward the clinic, Andy said, "You're a good teacher, Gina. I learned a lot last night." He smiled over at her. "You know, I was sure that I would make a fool of myself in the class. When I saw that you were the teacher, it made it even worse. I thought for sure you'd be rolling on the floor with laughter as I tried to get my fingers to find the right keys. Instead, you made it so we could all experiment and discover for ourselves where everything was. I can't wait for my next lesson."

Knowing that made Gina feel good.

"If I get time," he continued, "I'm going to try to practice on our office computer. Would you believe that even my father is a new age man? He and Caroline use the computer for orders and keeping track of the business. Dad even surfs the Internet."

When they reached the clinic, Andy gave Gina a card with his cell phone number on it. "Let me know whether Mel's car is fixed. If it isn't, I'll pick you and the kittens up and take you home. But you might have to wait at the clinic for a few minutes if I'm held up."

Andy lifted the kittens' cage into the clinic and set them on the counter of Gina's office area. When Gina hurried through the back of the clinic to hang up her coat and put her lunch in the fridge, Andy took a tape measure out of his pocket and checked the dimensions of the kitten's cage. He had just snapped the tape shut and stuffed it in his pocket when Gina returned. Immediately, Andy began to play with one of the kittens. It was the black one with the white tip on his tail. He was by far the most adventurous of the three.

Gina came over to watch the kitten swat at Andy's finger. "What have you called him?" he asked.

"Midnight."

Andy pulled a face at that.

Gina frowned. "You don't think that's a suitable name for a cat?"

"Well, can you imagine calling 'here, Midnight, here Midnight'?"

Gina laughed. "You've got a point. Okay. You get to choose a name. By the next time I see you."

Andy worked all morning at Carolyn's project. Although all three Thompson sons had their own trades and worked independently when it suited them, they also worked as part of Thompson Builders and Renovators. Carolyn, who had studied for a while to be an architect and who was a master carpenter, had the wider knowledge. Now that Jim Thompson was semi-retired, it naturally fell on her to negotiate projects and supervise their completion.

Today, Andy had to confirm what Carolyn had discovered. The century home they had been hired to renovate had a mediocre rewiring job done by someone in the past. To meet the safety codes, the place would have to be entirely rewired.

Over lunch, Andy discussed his findings with his sister. He watched her now as she ate a very nutritious lunch: pita wraps with vegetable filling, a shiny apple, and some very delicious looking oatmeal cookies.

He couldn't resist observing, "Since when have you taken to healthy lunches, Caro? You've eaten cheese slices in brown bread for as long as I can remember."

Carolyn took a bite of one of the cookies and then took pity on him and offered him one. "David has taken to cooking. He claims it takes his mind off mathematics long enough for him to formulate an answer to any problem he's posed. He's turning out to be a good cook too," she said proudly.

Andy sat back and enjoyed the cookie while watching his sister. She had always been lovely with her clear skin and long dark hair, but since her marriage to David, there was an added glow that bespoke great happiness. Her blue eyes, so like his own, had a new radiance when she spoke of her husband.

"How's work going over at the clinic?" she asked.

"I'm almost ready for the equipment to arrive. Merry says the manufacturers have promised one-day delivery the minute I'm ready. I certainly plan to have everything completed before Dan and Cindy return. By the way, how's the work coming on Cindy's tearoom? Shouldn't it almost be finished?"

"I made it a priority to get the upstairs apartment in the house done first." Carolyn replied. "Dan and Cindy can move in the minute they come home. I think it's a good thing they decided to delay their wedding until the end of March. It's meant that they could go away with peace of mind. When they return, Cindy can concentrate on getting the tearoom ready. Also, it allowed her brother to come home from England for the wedding. How's Merry managing?"

"Just fine. Oh, by the way, the ground fault switch in the bathroom at Cindy's parent's house has gone. Merry asked if I'd go over to fix it tonight."

Just then, Carolyn's pager rang. She took a message from her father, and after hanging up, she said, "Dad's fixed up the bicycle for Gina. He says he'll deliver it to the clinic in time for Gina to ride it home since you're busy out here."

When Andy made no effort to explain and just started to pack up his lunch, Carolyn said, accusingly, "Tease."

"Moi?"

She threw some tinfoil that had wrapped her pita at him. "C'mon. What's up?"

Grinning, Andy said, "Gina had kittens."

"An-dy," she laughed. "Quit fooling around. What is this about kittens?"

Having had his fun, Andy said, "Someone left a box of kittens outside the clinic. I found them. They're hardly old enough to walk around. Gina offered to look after them. That means she has to take them back and forth from work until they're old enough to manage by themselves."

"How many kittens?"

"Three. Want one?"

"You jest. Two young dogs and one cat are quite enough, thank you."

"How is Gina going to manage the kittens on a bicycle?"

"Dad made a box to fit on the back of your old bike." Looking at Carolyn, he said, "I presume that was alright. I understand you and David have new racers."

"Sure. Gina's welcome to it."

As she stood and packed up her lunch, Andy lingered. "Did you know that Gina is living alone in that old story-and-a-half house on Elm Street? The one that's fourth from the lake?"

"Old Miss Davidson's place?"

"You know it?"

"Sure. I've been in there. Community Care asked me to go in there and check the floor in the main room. Some of the boards had heaved. They were afraid she would trip. I fixed them. Surely, work has been done on that house since then? How come Gina is there?"

Andy explained about Gina's grandmother and expressed his concern about the wiring. "Dad said something about government funding for repair of heritage houses. Maybe something can be done. She's saving to have it rewired, but that could take ages."

With that, they went about their individual tasks, but Carolyn kept thinking about her brother. It was really good to have him taking an interest in others. It was so long since he'd thought about anything but his music.

Gina was just waiting for the last patient to leave when she saw a van drive into the parking lot. She recognized the tall, white-haired man who got out of it immediately. It was Andy's father.

When he came in, she greeted him. "Hi, Mr. Thompson. I'm sorry, but Andy isn't here."

"That's okay, my dear," he said. "It's you I've come to see. I understand you have a new family."

Beaming proudly, Gina pointed to a large cage on a stand in the corner. In it, the black kitten was attempting to pounce on a small ball of paper someone had put in the cage while the little Persian and the orange tabby were piled together, sound asleep.

"I understand that you plan to take them back and forth from home on a bicycle." Looking at the cage, Jim said, "Surely not in that big cage?"

Lifting up a smaller cage, Gina said, "No. I thought they could travel in this one. I think I could strap it on the back of a bicycle."

"Can you leave the desk for a minute? I've something to show you in the van."

Gina looked intrigued. "Sure. Just a minute. I've got to make sure someone answers the phone." Calling through to the back, she asked one of the technicians to take the calls and then headed out the door.

It had rained the night before, a good steady spring rain. Now the late afternoon sun picked up a hint of soft green that had suddenly appeared on the grass and the faint wash of greens, and even pinks, that touched the trees. They both stood for a minute on the clinic steps and breathed the warm air. "Spring at last," Jim said. "I thought it would never come."

Gina followed him out to the van, wondering what he

could have for her. He opened the door and reached in to pull out a bicycle. Over the back wheel a box had been fastened, just the size of the kitten's traveling cage. "This is Carolyn's old bicycle. Andy and I thought you might as well have it. It was gathering dust in the basement. I made the box from measurements Andy took this morning. Here, try it."

Gina looked at him and then back at the bike. "It's beautiful," she whispered. "But doesn't Carolyn mind?"

"Carolyn and David have new racers."

Jim was surprised to see a shimmer of tears in Gina's eyes. Her hands trembled as she took the handlebars of the bike. "That's very kind of you. Thank you."

Then, giving Jim a breathtaking smile, she stepped on the pedal, gave the bike a shove and heaved herself onto the saddle. With a huge grin on her face, she wheeled the bike along the front path of the clinic and down to the road and back. Coming to a stop, she said, "It's perfect." Checking the box, she noticed that it even had straps to hold the carrier.

Jim reached into the van and brought out a parcel. "My housekeeper made a waterproof cover to fit over the traveling case. Let's go and try it for size. When you're ready to leave, I'll drive behind you just to make sure that the cage is balanced."

Merry stood in the kitchen doorway, shaking her head with amusement as she watched the action in the next room. In the center of the living room floor, her four-year-old son, Michael, and her housekeeper's younger son, Peter, were playing with a battery-driven train set. Not only could the boys send the train around its track past a station, over a bridge, by a field, and through a village, but they could also drive their small cars and trucks along a road that crossed the train tracks several times. The unit was cleverly set up so that if the boys approached the track with their vehicles when the train was near, warning signals would come on and the train would automatically come to a stop. There were other twists to the ingenious device. A cow could be made to cross the tracks from the farmer's field causing the approaching train to blow its whistle.

Sitting on the floor with the two boys was quiet, reserved Andrew Thompson, revving his car along the road much to the delight of the boys. Michael flopped back on the floor holding his sides with laughter as Peter made the cow cross the railroad line before the car had a chance to trigger the warnings. Andy made screeching noises as he brought his vehicle to a stop.

The game finally turned into a bit of roughhousing. Michael started to drive his car up over Andy's arm, and Andy drove his truck over Peter's stomach. In minutes, both boys were throwing themselves on Andy.

Glancing at her watch, Merry saw that it was past their bedtime. Andy must have seen this, because he suddenly rolled away from them and reached for a toy ukulele the boys had been playing with earlier and had left by a chair. Sitting up, he began to strum the strings.

"Okay, boys. I'm all played out. How would you like to hear a song I'm making up? So far, I've only got part of it written. Maybe you could tell me if you like it."

The boys weren't so sure that they wanted to stop their fun, but Merry stepped in and said, "We can be the audience. Come and sit on the chesterfield with me and we'll listen.

Surprisingly, the boys did so without complaining. Obviously, Andy could do no wrong.

Andy stayed on the floor and held the little ukulele to his chest. He tuned it for a moment; then he began to sing softly,

"A yellow bird sat on an orange cat's head.
" 'I wonder what's above,' the orange cat said."

Andy stopped and asked, "Can you guess what the orange cat said?"

Michael guessed, "What's on my head?"

Peter chimed in, "Maybe he thinks it's a hat."

Andy ran his fingers over the string. "Let's find out what the cat said." Andy started the song again.

"A yellow bird sat on an orange cat's head.
" 'I wonder what's above?' the orange cat said.
" 'Something good to eat.
" 'Something good to crunch.
" 'What do you think?
" 'Will it make a good lunch?' "

The boys immediately called, "No."

Peter said, "The bird's not lunch."

"What should the cat have for lunch?" asked Andy.

"Cats eat mice," explained Michael.

"Oh dear," said Andy. "I guess I'll have to think of another verse for the song. Do you want to sing this verse with me again?"

The boys nodded and sang each line after Andy sang it. Then Andy began to sing a soft melody about going to bed. The boys weren't fooled. They looked at Merry to see if their hero was actually joining forces with her. She looked at her watch again and said softly when he finished, "It's long after bedtime. Who can get in his bed first?"

The boys thought about this challenge for a split second and then they were off. Just as Michael was about to disappear up the stairs, he stuck his head back and said, "Good night, Andy."

Not to be undone, Peter called, " 'Night, Andy."

Andy smiled at Merry. "They're great little guys." Standing up, Andy said, "Guess I'll be going. Go ahead and see them to bed."

Merry hesitated for a moment. "Would you mind staying for a coffee? I have a problem you might be able to help me with. I'll be right back."

As Andy listened to the sounds of the boys going to bed, he wondered what Merry's problem was. She probably wanted help with a wiring problem at the clinic.

Andy watched Merry as she poured out mugs of coffee and brought a plate of cookies to the table. Tonight she was wearing jeans and a bulky sweatshirt, a far cry from the white lab coat she wore at the clinic. She smiled at him as she handed him a mug of coffee. "It was nice of you to play with the boys. I know they miss spending time with a man."

"They're great little boys, both of them."

Merry nodded in agreement. "I'm so fortunate to have found Ruth with her little boy. She has a good head on her shoulders. She doesn't spoil the boys. At the same time, she makes sure they know they're loved."

"I imagine that working for you has been a godsend for Ruth. I know her mother could not have looked after Peter much longer. And Ruth would have found it very hard to make ends meet without a job. Being a very young widow is not an easy thing." Then, a bit embarrassed, Andy said, "Of course, you'd know about that."

"I was in a much better situation to handle life without my husband than Ruth. I was older and had worked in our practice long enough to know that I could always manage financially. Ruth and her husband were barely out of their teens when he died."

Then, shaking her shoulders as if to rid herself of past tragedies, she said, "I wondered if you might be able to give me some advice. I have about two months to find a house to buy or rent. I would like it to be big enough to allow Ruth and Peter to stay with me. I suppose, in the best of all worlds, a house with a granny flat or apartment in it would be ideal. Then, Ruth could have some privacy and create her own home."

"You know, I usually have an idea about houses coming up for sale in town just because the tradesmen talk. However, right at this moment, I can't think of any place."

He watched Merry's shoulders slump. And then she looked at him and smiled wryly. "Well, I shouldn't expect everything to come as easily as finding a practice here. I was lucky to know Dan from college."

Andy was still thinking about the problem. "The person who is most likely to know is Carolyn. I'll ask her for you, if you like."

"How about real estate agents? Can you recommend anyone?"

"People speak highly of Art Cramer. He has an office on Main Street. Why don't you speak to him?"

They were both silent for a moment, sipping their coffee. Looking up, Andy caught an expression on Merry's face that he could only interpret as desolate. He knew the feeling too

well to ignore it. Without thinking, he responded to her pain.
"You miss your husband very much, don't you?" he said
softly.

He watched her hands whiten as she gripped her cup.
Then, with a shaky sigh, she said, "Most of the time, I'm all
right. It's just now, when I think of creating a new home, that
I miss him so much." Then, looking at him out of her clear
blue eyes, she added, "But then, I think you know what I'm
feeling."

Andy felt himself slipping back into his habit of distanc-
ing himself from his own heartbreak. For once, it didn't
seem a satisfactory way to deal with life. He forced himself
to say, "I was married for only a few years. We were very
young, like Ruth and her Joe. My wife, Kelly, was struck
with a fast-acting leukemia. She was gone in months."

Merry reached out and touched his hand. He hadn't
shared his grief with anyone, not even his very close family,
not until this very moment. And Merry's touch seemed to re-
lease the pain he'd carried around.

Merry let go of his hand and said, "I think you're beginning to face the world again, Andy. You should start to look
around for a nice young woman to start a new life with together. You're a father waiting to happen."

Then, getting up, Merry poured more coffee into their
mugs. With a sigh, she said, "I'm a great one to give advice.
I suppose in time I'll be ready to try to build a new relationship. But right now, all I seem to be able to handle is work.
This business of finding a new home is almost more than I
can deal with."

And watching her as she briskly shoved the plate of cookies between them, Andy thought about what she had just
said. He did enjoy being with the boys. He did want a son or

daughter of his own. He should look for someone to share his life with again. Using Merry's son as a surrogate child was not the answer to his problem.

"What do you think of Gina's kittens?" Merry asked.

Thankful that she had changed the subject, Andy was all too glad to discuss them. "My Dad fixed up Carolyn's old bicycle and built a container so that she can take the kittens back and forth from the clinic to the house each day until they're old enough to live alone." And then, as an afterthought, he said, "Did you realize that Gina is living in one of the oldest houses in town over on Elm Street? Her grandmother left it to her. I took her home with the kittens and saw the inside. I'm very worried about the wiring in the place. Fortunately, she's had the sense not to overload the system."

Merry couldn't help but slip into her old tendency to play Cupid. "Do you think there's any way you can help her?"

"My Dad thinks there's a government program that assists people living in historical houses. He's going to look into it."

"Is there any way *you* could help her?" Merry emphasized.

She watched Andy mull this idea over. He certainly wanted Gina to have a safe place, but he hadn't thought of going in and offering to do the work for her. That seemed just a little like interfering, like stepping out of the lifestyle he had grown used to. A lifestyle that he now realized had become very inwardly focused.

"Maybe," he said to her. "We'll see what my father comes up with."

With that, he said, "I'd better get going. Thanks for the coffee and cookies."

Chapter Four

It really felt like spring on Thursday morning. The sun caught the pastel tints of swollen buds and released the warm smell of thawing earth. Already, the spikes of tulip and daffodil leaves were thrusting up through dried leaves to reach the sun's rays.

Andy decided to check at Gina's just in case she needed a ride, but when he reached her house, he found that she had already left. As he walked back to his van, he noticed the odd spear of green sticking out of the leaves that had blown up against the house and sidewalk. It looked, he thought, as if Gina had the makings of a garden. Then he remembered something from his childhood. On the way to the beach at the end of the street he had ridden his bike past Miss Davidson's. He remembered the flowers that had edged her walk and the glimpses of the garden behind the house. He wondered if Gina intended to try and revive it.

He heard laughter when he entered the clinic. When he stepped into the reception area, he found Gina, Mel, and

Merry on their hands and knees, reaching under chairs. Gina glanced up when she heard him in the doorway. "Close the door quickly," she warned. "Mel and I made the mistake of letting the kittens out of the cage for a few moments. Merry startled them when she came in, and they scattered under the furniture."

Putting down his tool box, Andy joined in the hunt. Right away, he spotted the orange kitten behind the stand that held the aquarium. Pointing, he said, "There's one over there."

Mel dived. "I've got him," he called and struggled to his feet with a wiggling ball of marmalade fur.

"Put him in the cage," ordered Merry as she reached under a chair and snagged the little tabby.

Intrigued, Andy watched as Gina nosed under another chair. Ignoring the distraction of her cute derriere, he checked behind the receptionist area. Sure enough, the black kitten was there, trying to shinny his way up onto the wheel of Gina's typing chair. "I've found Midnight," he called.

Gina rushed around the counter to take her wayward charge. Eyes sparkling and cheeks glowing from the fun of the chase, she said, "You called him Midnight. I told you that would make a good name." Holding out her hands, she said, "Let me have him and I'll put him back in his cage."

Andy watched as she held the small creature to her cheek and crooned, "You little rascal. Since when can you run so fast?" Something about the receptionist and kitten touched him, warmed some area around his heart that had been frozen in the past. Shaking off the sensation, Andy hurried back to finish the wiring. Tomorrow, Merry could arrange for the equipment to be ordered for Monday or Tuesday.

* * *

By closing time, there was a soft warm rain washing away the last vestiges of the winter. Following the last client to the door and locking it, Gina felt that she could see the grass growing as she watched. Spring amazed her. It always seemed to come so fast. Everything seemed greener than it had that morning.

As she returned to her desk, Andy came through from the back, his toolbox in hand. Instead of heading for the door, he came over to the counter. For a minute, he hovered, and Gina wasn't quite sure what he was waiting for.

"Something I can do for you, Andy?" she asked.

He fidgeted with a flyer on the counter then finally said, "Would you like to do a trade? Fifteen minutes of review on your computer for a ride home in a nice, warm van."

Gina had no problem with that. It certainly would be a wet ride home unless, of course, Mel was going that way. Deciding that she would be glad to help Andy at any time since he had been so good to her, she agreed.

"Come back here and take my chair."

He grinned at her self-consciously and headed around to her chair. "I have to admit that I feel all thumbs when I sit down before a keyboard."

Quite enjoying the sensation of being the one who was helping rather than the one who was being helped, she said, "Do you remember how to turn on the computer?"

Andy gave her a look to see if she was teasing. "Certainly. Watch." With a flourish, he reached over and turned on the switch.

They waited while the screen lit up. Immediately, it asked for a password. Gina reached in front of Andy and he was again aware of her fragrance. Even more immediate was the brush of a dark curl against his face as she entered the numbers and letters. It was all Andy could do to keep from leaning into the silky dark mass and inhaling the rich scent. *Hold on, buddy,* he thought. *You're here to practice. Keep your mind on the computer.*

Gina sat back in the chair beside him and waited.

Feeling very self-conscious, Andy proceeded to click the mouse on the start symbol. A list of words appeared. For a moment, he panicked. Which one to use? His fingers hovered.

Observing his hesitation, Gina said, "Think for a moment. What did you do in class? Shut your eyes and remember."

She was right. As soon as he put himself back into the lesson, the steps became clear. Frowning with concentration, he began to follow the steps he'd learned.

Gina was delighted. "Fantastic. You haven't forgotten a thing."

Turning toward her, Andy said, "I want to type up one of my short songs."

"Go ahead," said Gina and left him happily hunting and pecking his way through his song.

While he worked, Gina tidied up the reception area, checked over the next day's appointments, and made notes to herself about things she needed to order, while at the same time keeping an eye on Andy.

She couldn't help but admire him. His long, dark, chestnut hair was swept back in a ponytail. It reminded her of the many heroes who had swept manfully through the romantic historical sagas she enjoyed. Peeking over at him, she realized he had lovely long eyelashes. *Oh, why is it always the men who have the eyelashes or the curly hair?* Although, she had to admit she had pretty good eyelashes herself, and she definitely had curly hair.

He straightened before the monitor and his action drew her attention to his long, strong back. It was . . . beautiful. Startled by this observation, Gina busied herself by hurrying over to the cage with the kittens and prodding their sleeping bodies with her finger until they woke and became curious. She distracted herself with their antics until Andy called. "Gina, would there be a program of typing lessons on your computer?"

Surprised she hadn't thought of it earlier, Gina hurried over. Of course there was. It came with the original computer package. Without thinking, she reached over and clicked the mouse. In doing so, she brushed Andy's body and was immediately aware of him. Taken aback, she looked at him only to find that he was returning her look, his eyes as startled as hers. She felt the tiny hairs on the back of her neck rise. She was unable to breathe or turn away. Time seemed suspended.

Then a kitten mewed and time restarted. They both looked away and she let her breath out. Trying to hide the tremor in her voice, she said, "See the top icon on the right. Click on that."

Immediately, the typing program appeared on the screen. Its instructions were easy to follow, and Andy turned to them.

Going back to the kittens, Gina busied herself by placing them in their traveling cage and trying to bring her emotions back under control. What had happened back there? She'd felt such a rush of feeling. Unlike anything she'd felt before.

That evening, Andy drove his van up the driveway to Gina's back door. She hopped out right away and ran to unlock the door. Andy opened the side of the van and lifted out her bicycle. After placing it next to the door, he went back and got the kittens. Following Gina, he entered the hallway of her house. Even though it was warm out, he found himself shivering. Had it been this cold all winter? How had she survived the discomfort?

Gina went to take the kittens from him but he shook his head. "Go ahead and get the fire on. I'll settle the kittens and bring in some more wood."

Gina eyed him nervously as he walked in with several armfuls of wood and put them in the old-fashioned bin by the stove. He seemed to have been untouched by the episode that afternoon, but she wasn't. All of a sudden, everything he did caught her attention. She noticed the droplets of moisture on his hair as he brought in the wood. She was fascinated by the careful way he arranged the wood in the wood box.

Unsure of herself, but grateful for his assistance, she asked, "Would you like a cup of coffee before you go?"

He hesitated for a moment and then said, "I'd love to, Gina, but my Dad and our housekeeper expect me home for supper any minute. Thanks, anyway."

As she closed the door on his back and heard the engine of the van, Gina couldn't keep from thinking that he couldn't get away from her fast enough. Whatever happened earlier must have been all in her head. Vowing to remember that, she proceeded to check on the fire and begin supper.

Andy slowed his van once he was out of Gina's driveway. Going down the street and around the corner, he pulled over and came to a stop. He needed time to think. There was no question in his mind about what had happened at the computer. He recognized the attraction that had hummed between Gina and himself. The question he needed to ask himself was whether he was ready to act.

He'd taken what he thought was a brotherly interest in Gina long before this recent trip to the clinic. As early as last winter, he'd noticed her, been interested in her activities. But this new awareness was much different. To be honest, it had been there since he'd walked into the clinic on April 1st.

Gina touched something in him. Then another thought crossed his mind. Had Gina even understood what had happened between them? Would she want to respond to it?

Andy started the van. He would just have to find out. The more he thought about it, the more he wanted to succeed.

While Andy and his dad did the supper dishes, he asked, "Did you ever track down the information about those funds for repairing heritage houses?"

Jim snapped his fingers. "I knew there was something I wanted to tell you. I found the information on the Internet. There is such a program. The government will pay forty percent of the cost, provided the owner can prove the house's age. It will be necessary to do some research to get the proof."

"I suppose the historical society might be a help," suggested Andy.

"I'm sure they would," replied his father. "We could also check at the registry office and search the title. The entire history of the house should be there."

"Good idea. I'm sure Gina could do that."

Jim studied his son for a moment. "You're taking quite an interest in this house of Gina's."

Andy was tempted to share his feelings about Gina with

his dad, but he hesitated. "I just worry that she might get into real trouble over there."

"I'll tell you what," said Jim. "I'll get the forms off the Internet. I'll also run the problem past Carolyn. She's been in the house."

The next morning, Jim Thompson located the information on the Internet and printed it off. He had just begun to read it over and highlight key facts when his daughter Carolyn walked into his office.

She came over to his desk and placed a file on it. "Here's the final info on the Bruce account. John Bruce said he'd like you to confirm the total I gave him so that he can submit the last payment."

Jim beamed. "I'll check it right away. I wish all our clients were as eager to pay their accounts."

He began to clear away the papers he'd been reading when something in them caught his daughter's eye. "Heritage houses?"

"I'm sure that Andy must have mentioned to you that Gina, the receptionist at the animal clinic, is living in that old house on Elm Street."

"Sure. We talked about it. I've been in that house at least once. I understand the wiring is bordering on dangerous."

"Well, Andy seems quite anxious to do something about it. He says that Gina has to depend on the wood stove. She's afraid to use the heaters for fear of starting a fire. I knew that at some time in the past I had read about a government program to assist owners upgrade historically important houses in their communities. I just found it."

Interested, Carolyn drew up a chair. "Can I take a glance at the papers?"

Jim waited while Carolyn scanned them. Finally, she looked up at him. "It says the house must be at least a hundred years old. They request a short history of the house if possible, a diagram of the house at present, possible building problems, and a plan for the particular renovation requested. It also asks for two separate estimates."

Jim thought for a moment before speaking. Finally, he said what was on his mind. "You know, Carolyn, Andy seems quite keen on helping Gina. I haven't seen him so interested in someone else's problems since Kelly died. I think we should give him all the support we can."

Carolyn frowned for a moment. "Do you think Andy is just anxious that the house is safe, or does he have a particular interest in Gina?"

"Does it matter? Just to see a smile on his face and a light in his eyes is such a relief."

Carolyn leaned over and touched her father's arm. "You're right. If Gina can bring him back to life, then I'm all for it.

They heard Andy's voice as he spoke to the housekeeper. A minute later, he walked into the office.

"I thought you were installing the new equipment at the clinic today," Carolyn said.

"The equipment didn't come as promised, so I'll have to install it on Monday. Too bad. I really wanted to have it in before Dan got back." Glancing at the papers on his father's desk, he said, "Have you got a new project for me to work on?"

Jim handed him the pages. "This is the information about the grants available for repairing heritage houses."

They waited while Andy looked them over. When he'd finished, he said, "I think we'd better find out about the house's history. Do you have any suggestions, Carolyn?"

"I thought a trip to the registration office might be useful. Those records usually show a house's history."

"I'd be glad to do that," said Jim. "I could use a project. Being semi-retired can get boring at times. Anyway, Nora and I were thinking about going to a movie in Smithboro. I'll ask her if she'd like to go early and do a search and then have supper before the movie."

Carolyn raised an eyebrow at this and looked over her father's head at her brother. He grinned back at his sister, then said, "I'd appreciate that, Dad. The sooner we get the info, the sooner Gina can make an application."

Just then, Nora came into the office. "I've just made fresh coffee and scones. Would you like some? If so, come into the kitchen when you're ready."

They couldn't agree fast enough. Nora was famous for her scones. Jim followed her out, a look of happy expectation on his face. Carolyn and Andy waited for a second. Carolyn whispered, "Do we have a romance here? You live with Dad, Andy. Is something going on?"

"Not that I know of. But now that I think of it, they're playing bridge together." Picking up the grant information, Andy headed for the door, then paused. "How would you feel about them getting together, Carolyn?"

With the sparkle in her eye of a dedicated Cupid, she said, "I'd love it."

It was only natural that the house should have a dream kitchen. It had become a standing joke that Carolyn couldn't resist upgrading it every time a new innovation hit the market. The latest had been new counters. The family tolerated her urge to upgrade since she had never destroyed the kitchen's atmosphere. It had always been the place where the family discussed their problems.

Nora had placed a large platter of warm scones on a large oak pedestal table and was just in the act of pouring coffee into mugs when Caroline and Andy entered.

"Mmm," said Caroline. "Those scones smell divine." Taking a chair, Caroline lifted a scone and placed it on her plate. "Butter and jam too. You are an angel."

Soon, they were all busily spreading jam and biting into the delicious pastry. As they ate, they discussed the grant application. Their major concern was the length of time it would take to get the funds.

"I don't like the idea of Gina using those heaters while we wait. It will soon be too uncomfortable to use that big range. She may be tempted to turn them on," said Andy.

"How about the other wiring?" asked Jim. "Has she had any trouble with the electrical outlets? I imagine they're in similarly bad shape."

"I doubt there's an outlet that *isn't* questionable. I don't think Gina's thought of that. Probably give her nightmares if she did."

"Well," said Carolyn. "I think we should get the application in the mail as soon as possible. I could go over and get the info to make a proper blueprint. I could also check the foundation and roof. I presume the insulation is made of old newspapers or anything else the original owners could pack into the walls. She might as well ask for everything, since I see the grant doesn't just apply to wiring."

Nora, who had listened to enough to the discussion to figure out what was needed, added, "I'm sure I can get the members of the historical society to give us a hand. I'll try Luke Junkin. He has researched a lot of the houses in the village."

Jim beamed at Nora. "That's a great idea."

Carolyn looked at Andy and grinned.

When they'd finished their scones and coffee, Andy stood up. "I think I'll take the grant application over to Gina." Glancing at his watch, he said, "I'll see if she's free to come for lunch. We can go over the details. By the way, when do you expect Dan and Cindy back?"

"Sunday evening," said Carolyn. "If you're not busy, maybe you could come over to their apartment after lunch. There's still a little wiring to be done. If you complete it, I think they could move in right away."

"Sure."

"Let's go," said Carolyn. With a mischievous glint in her eye, she added, "Maybe I'll join you and Gina for lunch."

Merry said, "If the Browns call, Gina, tell them Fluffy came through her operation successfully. They can pick her up any time after three-thirty."

Merry waited while Gina made a note of the message, then asked, "Any word about the new equipment?"

Gina shook her head. "They promised to phone early this afternoon."

Just then, she heard the outside door of the clinic. Glancing at her watch, she saw that it was almost twelve. Hopefully, this wasn't going to be an emergency. Most people knew that, although there was someone around, they did not take appointments over the lunch hour. To her surprise, Andy stepped into the waiting room.

Merry said, "I thought that you weren't coming back until Monday. They still haven't phoned back about the time they intend to bring the ultrasound."

"I didn't come about the ultrasound. I came to see if Gina could be spared for lunch."

Gina's eyes flew to his and then away again. Lunch! Why would he want to take her to lunch?

As if she'd asked the question out loud, Andy explained. "I've found a way for you to afford to fix the wiring in your house. There's a government program available and I think your house qualifies."

Gina didn't quite take in everything he's said. "Government program?"

"Yes. I'll explain everything over lunch."

Before Gina could think of a reason for not going to lunch with the tall, confident man standing in front of her, Merry said, "I'll cover for you, Gina. If it gets busy, Mel can give me a hand."

"Great," said Andy and sent Merry one of those smiles guaranteed to make grown women melt on the spot. *Save those smiles for Gina*, Merry thought.

"Go ahead, Gina," she urged.

Feeling very self-conscious, Gina mumbled, "Thanks, Merry. I'll just freshen up. I'll be out in a minute, Andy."

While he waited, Andy wandered over to the kittens. "They're really getting around now. Look at Midnight. He's my favorite."

The black kitten was pouncing on his small, orange sister's tail. "By the way," Andy asked Merry. "Did you get in touch with Art Cramer about a house?"

"I have an appointment with him this evening. But he didn't sound too encouraging. I never anticipated there would be such a scarcity of places. Silly of me."

"I asked Dad and Carolyn to keep an ear out for anyone moving. My brothers will do the same. Don't worry."

At that moment, Gina stepped into the waiting room. She

looked at Andy and then quickly away. It was silly to feel self-conscious, but she did. Yesterday's moment was still with her. But then, she thought of what Andy had just told her. He thought there was a way to pay for her house's wiring. That would be a small miracle.

The first person Gina saw when she stepped into the restaurant was Carolyn, sitting alone at a table. When Carolyn saw her, she smiled and waved them over. Gina's first reaction was relief. Now she wouldn't have to be the only person at the table with Andy. At that moment, he touched her arm, steering her toward Carolyn.

Andy pulled a chair out for her beside his sister and then took the one across from her. Raising his eyebrow at his sister, he said dryly, "Glad you could make it, Carolyn."

She slanted an innocent, blue-eyed look that he recognized. She was enjoying the situation. He gave her back one of his best brotherly squints, warning her to watch her step.

Picking up the menu, she said casually, "You treating, big brother?"

Andy almost took the bait. He had to bite back the retort that he'd asked Gina for lunch, not her. Just as casually, he answered. "Of course."

"Well, then. Since this place has the best fish and chips in the area, I intend to have them."

"Gina?"

"I'd like fish and chips, too."

"That makes three of us," said Andy. "Good. While we're waiting for them, we can go over the grant application."

Gina interrupted. "Hold on, Andy. Explain to me what this is all about. What kind of application? What kind of grant?"

At that point, the waitress took their order. When she left, Andy explained. "I was telling my Dad about the wiring in your house. He remembered reading about a government program that paid part of the cost of updating century homes so that they were safe. Since our company does a lot of renovations on old houses, he was interested.

"He found the information on the Internet and showed it to Carolyn and myself. We think it's just the program to help you."

Andy got out the papers. "There are a number of things we have to do before we send in the application. First, we have to get proof of the age of the house. My dad is going to look after that."

"But your dad has been so kind to me already, fixing up the bicycle," said Gina. Then, remembering that the bike belonged to Carolyn, Gina said, "I didn't thank you for the bike, Carolyn. I can't tell you how much I appreciate it."

Carolyn shrugged. "You're welcome to it. Dad and his housekeeper, Nora, enjoyed fixing it up. And they're looking forward to searching out your house's history. They're going to check in the registry office. Also, Nora's a member of the historical society, and she's going to ask the members if they can give her any information."

"But why would they want spend their time doing that?"

Caroline explained. "My Dad is semi-retired now. I think he was glad to find something new to do. And he likes doing things with Nora, our housekeeper. I hope you don't mind."

Put like that, what could Gina say? "Of course I don't mind. I really appreciate what they're doing."

Andy continued. "They also want an inspection of the house. Carolyn is qualified to do that. And Carolyn can draft us a blueprint. I think we should ask for as much assistance as possible. They may allow money for other things beside the wiring. However, we'll stress the wiring as being the first priority."

Gina didn't know what to say. These two very competent people were talking so casually about what seemed to her to be a major effort, costing a small fortune. She fiddled with her fork while she tried to find the words to express her concern.

Finally, she said, "I appreciate all that you're doing, but you don't understand; I simply can't afford all this work. I've only got a little bit saved. It's going to take me ages to get enough money to do the work, even with the grant."

Andy reached over and stilled the hand that was turning the fork over and over. "Gina. You cannot live in that house the way it is. It's unsafe. Just walking around the other night, I saw enough wiring problems to give me nightmares. Don't worry. We're not going to do it all at once. We'll start with the safety issues at first. We'll work out something. I promise."

The waitress came with their plates of crispy fish and homemade chips. Grabbing a french fry from her plate, Carolyn nibbled on the end of it. "These are heavenly, Andy. It was so nice of you to think of this place."

Andy rolled his eyes at his sister and then turned back to Gina. He should have anticipated that their enthusiasm would overwhelm her. She was sitting there looking at her plate of food as if it was the enemy. Unable to stand her apparent misery, he took a chip from her plate and held it to her lips. "Come on, Gina. They're the best chips in the country. Try one."

She glanced up at him and was swamped by the warmth of his expression. Suddenly, she felt that, together, they might just have the answer to her problems. Dollar-wise, it didn't make sense. But she had to put her trust somewhere.

She leaned forward and nibbled on the chip. "You're right. It's delicious." For a while, they ate, talking casually about the goings-on about town; the fact that people would soon be putting their boats in the lake below the falls, that the tennis club would start in a few weeks, and that before they knew it, stores would be selling flowers. Then, conversation returned to more specific tasks.

Carolyn said, "I still have quite a bit of work to do on Dan and Cindy's apartment; some trim and handles in the kitchen and the final painting of the cupboards. If I could finish by noon tomorrow, maybe I could get over to your place in the afternoon, Gina."

Gina caught her breath. Carolyn was thinking of starting so soon! Even before she could get her head around the idea that the work might actually happen. For a few seconds, she felt her life was spinning out of control. Then she had an idea. One that would let her feel more a part of things.

"I could come over and help with the painting. I did my own kitchen cupboards just a few months ago. I'd like to help. It would be nice for Cindy and Dan to find their apartment ready to move into."

Carolyn grinned. "You'll never hear me saying no to help." Turning to Andy, Carolyn continued, "You have some wiring to do tomorrow at the apartment also. If we all worked in the morning, then maybe we could tackle Gina's place in the afternoon." As an afterthought, Carolyn asked Gina, "You don't have to work at the clinic on Saturdays?"

Gina shook her head. "Shirley Browning comes in on the weekends. What time would you like me?"

"Let's start at nine."

Andy said quietly, "I'll pick you up, if you like." He left money to cover the meal and tip and said to Gina, "I'd better get you back. See you over at the apartment in a few minutes, Caro."

When they got into Andy's van, he studied Gina for a minute. She was sitting calmly enough, but her hands gave her away. She was gripping them so hard that her fingers were positively white. He wanted to take them and warm them, make them relax.

"You're worrying, aren't you, Gina?" he said. "I promise you that we won't do anything you feel uncomfortable with. If we get carried away, you just say so."

Gina gave him a tentative smile and seemed to relax. When they got back to the animal clinic, Andy said, "See you at eight forty-five tomorrow morning."

If anyone had told me that I'd be kneeling with my head in Dan Jameson's kitchen cupboard a few weeks ago, I would have said that they were crazy. Gina poked the brush in a difficult corner and completed the second coat of the last cupboard beneath the counter. Pulling her head out of it, she sat back on her heels and admired her handiwork. The cupboards were a soft peach that Cindy had chosen to set off the light-colored refinished hardwood floor that covered the second floor. It was an unusual choice, Gina thought, but absolutely right. The counters were cream, as was the area under the upper cupboards.

Gina said to Carolyn, who was working at the inside of

the upper cupboards, "I really like the colors Cindy chose. The room faces the north. This color will really help make the kitchen seem warm." Then, another idea hit her. "She needs a plant. Do you think she'd mind if I got them one? The green would really set off the peach."

Carolyn pulled her head out of the cupboard and looked down at Gina thoughtfully. "I'm sure she'd be pleased."

Gina couldn't help saying, "I know you know what I did to Dan and Cindy. I can't tell you how sorry I am I did it. I really want them to be happy." She added, "I think I must have been very lonely and very insecure. I'm not really such a nasty person."

Then Carolyn did a completely unexpected thing. She gave Gina a big hug. "Quit worrying about it. We all make mistakes. The thing is, you told Dan in the end." Putting down her brush, she turned to her brother who had been plugging the stove into the new outlet he'd just installed, "Andy, can we use the stove now? I've just finished my last cupboard."

"Sure," he answered. "Put on the teakettle."

At that moment, they heard the doorbell ring downstairs. "Lunch," called Carolyn. Gina was surprised. She'd assumed that they'd pick up something at the local coffee shop. She heard Carolyn hurrying down the stairs to the front door. Moments later, voices and footsteps came hurrying back up. The first person to enter the kitchen was David, Carolyn's tall, curly-headed husband, carrying an armful of light plastic deck chairs. He was followed by Carolyn's father and a lady Gina didn't know. Finally, Carolyn entered, carrying a basket of food.

Turning to Gina, she said, "Here, help me put the food on the counter while I move our brushes and paint." Over her shoulder, she called to everyone, "The outside of the cupboards are dry, but try not to touch them. They need a little longer to harden. The insides are wet."

Gina took the basket and placed it on the counter. Jim Thompson came in and handed her another. He called over a grey haired woman whose pleasant smile touched Gina. "Meet Nora Philips," Jim said. "Thanks to her, Andy and I eat well and are kept neat and tidy."

"I had help," Nora explained. "David made desert."

David bowed at that compliment and started to set up a card table that seemed to appear from nowhere. From one of the containers, he lifted out paper plates and plastic mugs. He topped that off with a large thermos of coffee.

"Ooh, coffee," Carolyn sighed. Going over to her husband, she gave him a big hug. "You're a genius."

Never one to miss an opportunity, David ended up kissing her. Andy groaned. "That's enough hanky-panky. Where's the food?"

In no time, the six of them were seated in a circle around the card table with their paper plates full of sandwiches, pickles, and celery. Talk was general, and Gina began to feel part of the group. Conversation turned to Merry's house problem when Andy asked if any of them had heard of a house that would be suitable for Merry.

"I certainly haven't heard of anything," said Carolyn.

"I did hear of a winterized cottage out on Ribbon Lake," said Jim. "But that's quite a drive from town. The cottage is very isolated. I can't see Merry wanting to be so far from her clients. One good snow storm in the winter could keep her from work. I'm not even sure whether the plough goes in there or whether it's a private road."

"She'd like to have a place big enough to have an apartment for Ruth and her little boy," Andy reminded them. "Too bad one of the old Victorian houses in town wasn't on the market. They'd be perfect. There's always room for an apartment in them. Look at the one I have on the third floor."

"Well," said Carolyn, "We'll keep our ears open. Maybe the real estate agents in town know something."

At that point, Carolyn picked up the container of cookies from the counter. "You must try some of David's cookies. They're out-of-this-world delicious."

Jim got up and wandered about the other rooms in the upstairs apartment. "You've done a good job here, Caro. The floors came up beautifully. I like the bathroom too. Who chose the tiles and fixtures?"

"Cindy. She's got a good eye for detail. If the rooms downstairs turn out as well, she's going to have a very attractive tearoom. When do you start work on that?"

"As soon as they get home."

Carolyn got a dreamy look on her face. "It's too bad we couldn't move all their things over here today. Or at least the essentials. It would be so nice to surprise them with the finished place."

Andy stood and began to clean up the paper plates. "Not a chance, dear sister. We already have plans for this afternoon. Dan and Cindy will stay in the apartment at the back of the clinic until they're ready to move their things."

Carolyn tossed her crumbled napkin at her brother. "You just don't have a romantic spirit."

"Thank goodness," Andy said. "We'd all have sore backs lugging beds and dressers up those stairs and end up putting them in the wrong places. Anyway, we're off to Gina's."

At those words, Gina's stomach tightened with nervousness. In just a few moments, they would all be at her place. What if they found that the house was legally unfit for habitation? Would they be obliged to report this to the building inspectors? Would she have to move out? Where would she go?

Shutting her eyes, she took a moment to take some big breaths. This had to stop. Her imagination was driving her wild. Of course, the house would be okay.

Suddenly, she was aware that Andy was beside her. She could sense his nearness without even turning her head. She could smell his aftershave. Without warning, he touched her arm and, to her horror, she jumped.

"Let's go, Gina, and get this over with."

Gina stood by the kittens' cage absentmindedly poking her finger in it and waiting for Midnight to attack. She was hovering. In her own house! She didn't know whether to laugh or cry. Upstairs, she could hear Carolyn and Andy walking about, shifting furniture, trying windows and tapping on walls. She supposed she should be with them, but what good would that do? The only things she knew about electricity were that you turned off the power if you wanted to repair a plug and that you shouldn't use a plug that sparked. She knew even less about house construction.

A few minutes later, she heard them coming down the small staircase that led into the kitchen. "You have a real treasure," said Carolyn enthusiastically. "This house is a classic example of what is known as a story-and-a-half. The Gothic window is typical, as are the windows on each side of the main entrance. Of course, some things have been added, as you know."

Gina's heart warmed with this praise. But it cooled again when Carolyn said, "I'm going to check all the wiring with Andy; then he can help me check the structural soundness of the house."

Trying desperately to gain some control over the situation, Gina asked, "Isn't there something I could do?"

"Of course," said Carolyn. Picking up her clipboard from the kitchen counter, she said, "If you could make a note of the important facts as we go around, it would save me writing them down. That way, we can work faster."

An hour later, Gina had filled three pages with facts. With each additional piece of information, Gina was more depressed. The wiring was appalling. The insulation sketchy and primitive, and the downstairs floor uneven and, in the odd place, downright dangerous. Fortunately, that section of floor had been in the part of the house Gina kept closed off.

In spite of herself, Gina sighed. Andy looked at her sharply and then said, "I think we're nearly finished here, but I could sure do with a cup of tea or coffee."

Taking the hint, Gina said, "I'll make tea, if you like. Come into the kitchen when you're finished."

Standing at the kitchen sink, Gina fought tears. Until today, she'd lived in a fool's paradise. Her home had seemed so wonderful to her. Oh, she knew improvements had to be made, but she'd never suspected how bad things were.

She had just finished making the tea and set out mugs when Carolyn and Andy came in. Quickly, she poured tea for them but, for the life of her, she couldn't smile. They chatted about the house's potential. *Potential.*

All that word meant to Gina was dollars and cents. Money she would never have.

She handed Carolyn a mug of tea and was rewarded with one of those smiles that genuinely warm the observer's heart, but it did nothing to melt the fear that was gripping Gina's.

"Thanks," said Carolyn. Then, as Gina handed Andy a mug and brought one to the table for herself, Carolyn added,

"We made really good time doing that inspection, thanks to you. I should be able to write up our findings tonight."

Andy had been watching Gina and realized that all was not well. She was pale and gripping her mug tightly. He was sure that at one point this afternoon he had caught the shimmer of tears in her eyes. Wasn't Gina happy that they were helping her? That they hoped to get her funds that would make it possible to live safely in the house? Then he remembered the panic he had seen in her eyes that morning. Was it possible that Carolyn and he were simply overwhelming her with detail? The expense must seem enormous.

He sipped his tea. Coffee was his preference but, he thought soberly, tea was much cheaper to serve. Then he had an idea. "Gina. You have no idea what a wonderful gift your grandmother gave you when she left you this house. It is a terrific investment. Its value will continue to grow over the years so that you will always have a nest egg when you need it."

He watched as Gina considered this. He thought he saw a little color return to her face. "And think of the fun you will have researching about these old houses and, over time, getting yours just the way you want. Look how much work you've done already in this room. You've captured the period perfectly."

Gina colored at little more at that, then finally found the courage to say what was on her mind. "I do love my house. I have had fun fixing it up. But . . ." At that, she looked down at her mug of tea, then up at them. "I had no idea that there was so much wrong with it. It sounds as if it could collapse at any moment or, at least, burst into flames."

Andy caught his sister's eye. This was their fault. They had been so enthusiastic about helping that they had forgotten that Gina could easily be discouraged by all their discoveries.

Carolyn was quick to pick up his concern. She said, "Your house is going to be fine. You should have seen our house when David first invited *Thompson Renovating* to take a look at it. Did you know that the ceiling plaster fell on him? You don't have any problem as serious as that."

Honesty required that Andy add, "Well, maybe the wiring is as serious, but that is easily dealt with."

What does easily dealt with mean? Gina wondered.

As if reading her mind, Andy said, "I'm positive you'll get the funding for this house. You fulfill all the requirements. But until it arrives, I think you and I could work out a business arrangement."

Doing math in her head and knowing that what she could save in a week wouldn't cover an hour of Andy's labor, she frowned, "A business arrangement?"

When Andy uttered the words *business arrangement*, he hadn't a clue what he meant. It had been an automatic response to her obvious distress. But suddenly, a full-blown fantasy filled his imagination. He saw himself sitting beside her as he mastered the computer. He would fix dangerous parts of the wiring for lessons! She could give him lessons on the computer.

He looked up and saw his sister watching him carefully. Ignoring the fact that he would probably be in for some teasing, he said, "I'll give you an hour of electrical service for every hour you give me computer instruction."

Andy watched while Gina mulled this over. She was no fool. He knew that she would not want charity. She was looking at her mug again and those deliciously long eyelashes were hiding their expression.

Then Carolyn piped up, "I didn't realize that you were studying computer, Andy. Am I ever glad! That will take some of the load off my shoulders."

Giving him a 'you owe me, brother dear' look, she demurely sipped her tea and waited.

Her remark seemed to be what Gina needed. Suddenly, her face was alive with enthusiasm. "I'd be glad to teach you if you're sure that seems a fair trade."

Standing too, Carolyn added, "Just think, in a few months, Andy, you'll be able to do this work on the computer."

A spring breeze warmed the earth as they stepped out into the garden behind the house. "Mmm, it smells marvelous," said Carolyn. "Would you happen to know where the lot line goes?"

Gina felt much better now. Without waiting for the others, she headed off over the lawn while calling over her shoulder. "My grandmother had the property surveyed several years before she died. I'll show you where the markers are."

In the end, Carolyn and Andy were both impressed. "The lot is huge," Andy remarked. "Far larger than the one our family's house stands on."

Walking about, Carolyn checked trees and shrubs. "There was a wonderful garden here in the past. You have lilacs and, look, a miniature apple tree." Pointing to a raised bed that ran possibly fifteen feet, she said, "This must be a perennial bed. Do you remember what it was like last summer?"

Gina was embarrassed. "You know, I've never had a garden. I didn't really know what to do with the plants that grew there last summer. I did try to weed them a little. I know that in June and July the garden was pretty."

"You should speak to my father," said Carolyn. "He loves gardening. He used to have wonderful beds of flowers before he developed a bad heart. My brothers and I have tried to look after his gardens, but I don't think we've done a very good job. I'm not sure whether he's thinking of gardening again now that his surgery has been so successful. Maybe helping with yours would be just what he needs."

When Gina looked doubtful, Andy said, "Let's just wait and see what Dad plans to do with his time now that he's feeling better."

When, it seemed, they had checked over every section of the property and made the appropriate notes, Carolyn hopped into her van and headed home. Andy checked his watch and saw that it was nearly supper time. His dad and Nora were going somewhere. The thought of going to an empty house and scrounging through the fridge didn't interest him.

He glanced over at Gina. She was watching Carolyn's van disappear up the street. This seemed as good a time as any to start getting to work and, more importantly, to get to know Gina.

When Gina turned to go into the house, he said, "I think I could start on the wiring tonight. That way, you might be able to give me a lesson Monday after work at the clinic. How about I go and get a pizza and bring it back? We could have it for supper and then I could work for a while."

Andy couldn't tell just exactly what Gina thought of this idea, but she was too polite to disagree. After deciding what should be on the pizza, he headed out.

When Andy returned with the pizza, he found that Gina had changed out of her work clothes. Tonight, she had on a pretty flowered blouse and fresh jeans. He noticed that she had also added tiny pearl earrings.

Dragging his attention back to more mundane things, Andy saw that she had set the table with place mats that picked up the rose color in the tiny pattern on the blue wall paper. White dishes were ready, and coffee was dripping through the maker, sending its fragrant aroma about the room.

Together they served up the pizza. Gina hadn't had an Italian father for nothing. She took a slice and bit into it with enthusiasm. It was delicious. Looking over at Andy, she saw him doing the same as he watched her. She couldn't help grinning. "That is one fabulous pizza. Thanks Andy."

Just as they were finished, Andy noticed a tiny string of cheese sticking to her lower lip. Fascinated, Andy watched her try to capture it with her tongue. When she had no success, he reached over and detached the piece of cheese from her lip; a lip that was soft and tempting.

For a moment, their glances held, and he watched as she nervously licked her lower lip. A log fell in the stove and broke the spell.

Oh, you are in serious trouble, thought Andy. Taking a gulp of his coffee, he turned his attention to his last bit of pizza and left Gina to struggle with hers on her own.

Although the pizza was delicious and had all her favorite toppings, Gina was glad when the meal was over. For a moment there, she had been startled by the touch of his finger on her lip. His blue-eyed look of concentration had engulfed her.

And now, instead of going off to do whatever electricians did when they were beginning a project, he was standing beside her at the sink, drying dishes. He was so close that she could actually feel the heat of his body and smell the faint scent of aftershave.

Trying to distract herself, she asked, "How will you start working on the house?"

"I'll have to put in a new power box with a 220 service. I can't believe it. This house is still wired on 110. And that," he paused, dipped his finger into the soap suds and plumped some bubbles on her nose, "will cost you at least a week of lessons."

Wrinkling her nose and trying to dry it off with the back of her wrist, she grinned. "I can see that I'm going to be working night and day. If you're not careful, you'll become so efficient on the computer that you'll have to do all the accounts for Thompson's Renovations by yourself." And then, quite unable to resist the temptation, she flicked soapsuds back at him.

The battle was on. He cupped a handful of suds. Giggling, she darted over to the other side of the table. He made a swipe at her, his suds bubbling off his hand in a series of little rainbow globes. She darted back and dipped some more. Not to be outdone, he grabbed the detergent bottle and squirted more into the dishwater. One swirl of his hand, and he was in business.

He watched as the tense girl of the afternoon dissolved into a giggling gamin, her dark eyes sparkling, her white teeth flashing. She darted behind the table again, and he began to stalk her.

"Girl who sprays bubbles must pay," he growled.

Laughing even harder, she replied, "Man with ponytail may find it soaked."

The game proceeded until, at last, he let her catch him and spread the bubbly mass over his head.

He surrendered. "Ponytail has had it. I give up."

He watched as she collapsed into a kitchen chair, laughing and holding her side. Andy couldn't remember when he'd ever laughed like that.

As Andy sorted out the tasks he needed to do and cleared out the space around the washer and dryer where he intended to put the power box, he realized that he felt happier than he had in years.

Chapter Five

Gina pedaled as slowly as she could to work. The day was just too lovely to rush. The air was full of bird song. The sun was catching the new green of the tree buds and finding the first brazen dandelion on a green verge.

Today the newlyweds would be back, ready to take up their lives together. Cindy would be anxious to start work on her tearoom. Gina hoped the menus would help.

Reaching the clinic, she put her bike in the stand and, loosening the kittens' cage, walked toward the entrance. As usual, she struggled with the door and the cage. Suddenly the weight of the door disappeared, and she almost fell into the waiting room. Getting her balance, she found herself looking into Cindy's laughing brown eyes. "I hear you have a new family. I can't wait to see them."

Gina couldn't resist slipping the cover off so that Cindy could admire the kittens.

Cindy chuckled as the three balls of fur tottered about while Gina carried them over to the larger cage. "They're so cute." She held the door of the larger cage open as Gina put the kittens into it. "May I hold one?" she asked.

When Gina nodded, Cindy picked up the little orange cat. In the two weeks Gina had had the kitten, it had grown steadier on its feet and considerably bolder. In the warmth of Cindy's hand, it began to purr.

At that moment, Merry walked through from the back. When she saw the kitten, she began to sing, *A yellow bird sat on an orange cat's head, "What's on my head," the orange cat said?*

Gina and Cindy both turned to Merry and stared. "What's that you're singing?" asked Cindy.

"It's a nursery rhyme Andy Thompson sang to the two boys the other night. He was just starting it. As I recall there were only about four lines done. The boys loved it."

"How's the house-hunting going?" Cindy inquired.

"Not well," Merry replied. "I saw Art Cramer, the real estate agent, and so far, he has nothing suitable. I'm really beginning to panic. When are you moving into your apartment above the tearoom?"

"Tonight we hope. We talked to Carolyn last night. She and David and her older brother, Mike, and his wife are going to help." Then, turning to Gina, she said, "I understand that Andy is having a lesson with you, after which he'll also help. Carolyn said that you would give us a hand too."

Responding again to Cindy's smile, Gina said, "It should be fun."

Gina had just decided that Andy was going to skip his lesson when he hurried in. "Don't pack up your computer yet, Ms. Falconi. I'm here to polish up my typing skills."

Throwing his coat over a waiting room chair, he headed around the counter. "Well, Teach, where do I start?"

Suddenly very aware of Andy in her small space, she hastily stood and held her chair for him. "Settle yourself right down here. See if you can figure out how to get the typing program going."

Andy looked at her blankly. "Me? Get the program going? You haven't taught us how to do that yet."

"Sure I have. Just think for a few moments. Review what you learned the other day."

He stared at the screen, then looked comically at her. "You're not going to help me, are you?"

"Nope," she said. "The answer to your problem is as clear as the nose on your face."

Sauntering over to the kitten's cage, she hummed as she teased Midnight through the wires with the tip of a pencil, while at the same time watching Andy surreptitiously. After giving her one very frustrated look, he settled back and stared at the computer. She could see that he was checking the keyboard and then the screen.

A dimple appeared in one cheek as he grimaced at the icons. A dimple she'd never noticed before. One just deep enough to invite a kiss.

A kiss. Where on earth had that thought come from? Annoyed with her wayward mind, she turned back to the kittens. Moments later, she heard him say "Yes!"

"You figured it out?"

He gave her one of those blinding Thompson smiles, his blue eyes sparkling with triumph. "You click on the program icon."

"That's right."

She watched as he clicked himself through the beginning

of the program. Then an expression she didn't quite trust crossed his face. He looked at her and, for some reason, she didn't quite believe his innocent expression when he said, "I think I need help putting my fingers on the keys."

She was ready to burst out laughing at that, but he stopped her in her tracks when he said, "C'mon, Teach. A bargain is a bargain." He beckoned to her and waited.

She walked around to the computer and asked him exactly what it was he couldn't do.

He explained, "I think my fingers are too big for the keys." She looked down at his hands hovering over the keys. There was nothing clumsy or too big about them. His fingers were long and elegant. Surprisingly, his nails were clean and carefully trimmed, not something she would have expected after a hard day's work. She looked at him and he returned the look with what could only be called bland innocence. An expression she didn't trust for a moment.

"If you were just to show me how my hands should sit on the keyboard, I'm sure I would be fine. I need to get some practice in before we eat and go over to the tearoom."

Mentally rolling her shining dark eyes, Gina gave in and, reaching over, took a hand. Not a good idea. Its warmth sizzled up her arm. Deciding that this was a dangerous game, she said, "Move over."

Taking the seat, she said, "Read to me what it says on the screen."

"Put your first and second finger of your left hand on D and F." She did so.

"Read me the next instruction."

"Put the first and second finger of your right hand on J and K." She demonstrated.

Standing, she said, "Now, Andy, I am sure a smart fellow

like you can do what little ol' me just did." Grinning, she added, "No more horsing around, Andy. Do the exercises. I'm taking the kittens' cage back to clean it out. Let me know when you can do that first exercise perfectly."

Gina carefully unwrapped the last glass and put it on the shelf.

"Here's another box of glassware," Andy said. "They're to go on the top shelf."

Andy placed the box at her feet. "If you unwrap each object, I'll place it on the shelf."

"How do you know the things go on the top?"

"Cindy told me. The box contains some family heirlooms. Beautiful English crystal goblets that belonged to an aunt of Cindy's."

"Okay".

Andy looked down and watched as she carefully unwrapped tissue from around an exquisitely fine-cut goblet. Holding it up to admire it, she whispered, "It's beautiful."

So are you, Andy thought. Her dark curls shone blue in the kitchen light. Her eyes glowed as she turned the goblet to catch its rainbow hues. She took his breath away.

Carefully, she handed it to him, and he placed it on the top shelf.

Much to Andy's disappointment, they were finished in no time. "We make a good team," he said and was pleased to see her blush. "I'll go and see what else I can find." Taking the box, he headed out of the kitchen.

Waiting for him to return, Gina began to cover another shelf with paper. She wondered if she dared go into one of the other rooms to discover whether there was something else she could do; something that wouldn't involve working with Andy Thompson. She found him far too interesting for her own good. She was just putting the shelf paper away when he came in whistling a tune and carrying a box over to a set of drawers.

He opened the box, and she could see that it contained long, thin bundles of newspaper. Knives and forks, she guessed, and when he opened one package, she saw that she was right.

"Before you put those away in the drawer, I think we'd better wash and dry them," she decided.

He turned toward her with a look of horror and held the package of newspaper before him as if to ward off evil. "You expect me to trust you near a sink of soapy water? After what you did to me?"

She couldn't help but giggle at his play acting.

"You mean you're afraid that you might get your ponytail all wet again?"

"Certainly. I prize my ponytail. It is rare among men. How many other men do you know that have such handsome locks?"

At that, she burst into laughter. "Locks. Since when are ponytails locks?"

"Well," he sniffed and turned on the water in the sink. "Mine is. You'll notice it has a slight wave at the end." With that, he poured detergent into the water. "I'm washing. There's no chance you're getting near the soapsuds. Dry, woman."

Still laughing, she took the towel, and they proceeded to work away at the cutlery until it was all washed, dried and put away in the plastic container in the top drawer.

Just as they were cleaning up, Cindy wandered through. "Oh, you angels. I had visions of having to wash all the cutlery before I could use it."

Without thinking, Gina said, "If you know where your dishes are, we could wash them and put them in the cupboards too."

"Would you? It would save so much time." When they nodded, she said, "Andy, I think they're downstairs in the front room. There are several boxes. I wrote 'dishes' clearly on them."

For a half an hour, they worked together. Gina felt herself relax. He was right; they did make a good team.

Downstairs, Cindy came upon Carolyn opening boxes. "Tell me, Carolyn. Has something happened since we were away? Your brother is upstairs with Gina washing the dishes. He was whistling a very happy tune, and Gina has a glow on her that would light a dark room."

Carolyn sat back on her heels. "I know. It's like a miracle. I was beginning to think that Andy was going to become a permanent hermit. Gina seems to have lit some kind of fire in him." Standing and brushing off her long legs, she added, "I'm holding my breath. Just praying that something comes of this."

Finally, everything in the boxes was unpacked. Carolyn and David had helped Dan and Cindy set up the bedroom suite so that they could stay in their own place that night. All that was left to come over was some living room furniture. They planned to move it the following night.

In spite of herself, Gina yawned. Glancing at her watch, she was surprised to see it was 10:00. She had to get home. She still wanted to glance over the material for the next day's computer lesson at the library.

She glanced around for Andy. After their typing lesson, he had insisted that she have supper with him at the tiny restaurant on Main Street. Now, she was hoping he would take her home.

A minute later, he came in from carrying out tied-up boxes for the recycling.

Glancing at his watch, he was surprised to see how late it was. Turning to Dan and Cindy, he said, "I'm sorry that I can't help tomorrow night. I have this mean teacher over at the library who won't let me skip my computer lesson."

When Cindy and Dan looked curious, he pointed to Gina. "Teach."

Grabbing her jacket, Gina laughed and said, "Let's get going. I still have to look over my lessons. Carolyn and David can explain."

Once they were settled in Andy's van, Gina observed, "On a nicer evening, we could have walked."

That pleased Andy. Did she realize that she was looking into the future, seeing them doing something together? A good sign. When they reached her place, he insisted on coming in. The house was cool. He wanted to start the fire for her, but she insisted that she would be fine. "What I need is sleep. I feel unusually tired tonight. I'm going to bed right away. I'll look over my lesson tomorrow at lunch. No typing lesson tomorrow. See you at seven, tomorrow night."

"I'll pick you up if you like." Leading him to the door, she said, "That would be great. Thanks for the ride home." He had no choice but to leave, but he waited outside the door until he heard the lock click shut.

The next evening, as Andy was making his way into the library with Gina, he noticed a black pickup drive up. Telling Gina to go ahead, he walked over to check it out.

Sure enough. It had the same slightly askew license plate he'd observed on the truck that had left the clinic just before he'd found the kittens.

A tall dark-haired guy swung out of the cab of the pickup, reached in to get some books, and headed toward Andy.

"Excuse me," said Andy trying hard to keep his tone ordinary rather than accusatory.

The fellow stopped and stood shivering in the damp evening air. Andy could see that he wasn't dressed very warmly. He had on worn jeans and a plaid shirt over a black t-shirt. He glanced around before saying, "You speaking to me?"

"Yes," answered Andy. "I think you left a box of kittens out by the steps of the animal clinic."

The man shivered again. "Can we talk inside?"

Well, at least he isn't denying it, thought Andy and followed him into the library. In fact, the man caught Andy off guard by stopping, turning to him, and offering his hand. "I'm Nick Mitchell."

Andy found himself responding to his firm grip. "Andy Thompson."

"I know. I've seen your truck around town."

Not willing to be sidetracked, Andy asked, "What about the kittens?"

"I found them in an old crate out behind my boarding house. They were crying and very cold. I looked around for their mother and unfortunately found her dead in the lane. She'd obviously been hit by a car. I sneaked the kittens into my room but realized quite quickly that I couldn't look after them. My landlady would have had them out in a moment. All I could do was make sure they were warm and pray they lived until morning when I could leave them at the clinic."

Nick looked down for a moment and then back up at

Andy. "I had to leave them outside the clinic. There was no way I could afford to pay for their care. I waited until I saw someone come out and then left. It must have been you. I figured you would hear them. They'd kept me awake all night." He paused and then asked, "What happened to them?"

"I noticed the box and took it in. The receptionist is taking care of the kittens. They're really quite cute now. They can walk about easily now and feed themselves."

"I'm relieved to hear that they're alright." Glancing at his watch, he said, "Look, I've got to go to class. Please thank everyone who looked after them, particularly the receptionist."

When Andy reached the class, everyone had their computers on and were busy following a sheet of instructions. Gina was busy answering a student's question, so he settled down at his own computer and got to work. He wasn't surprised when Gina left him to his own devices. After all, she'd answered most of his questions over the past few days. What pleased him most was that his fingers felt more comfortable on the keyboard. Of course, he couldn't touch-type yet, but somehow, his fingers seemed to have adjusted to the size of the keyboard and were frequently over the right key.

When the class came to an end, some of the students decided to go and have a coffee. Andy looked at Gina to see if she was interested, but she shook her head. "I need an early night. I'm really beat. Don't let me stop you from going."

Far more interested in spending time with Gina than going for coffee, Andy said, "I wouldn't mind an early night either. I'll drop you off at the house and head home."

Chapter Six

When Gina awoke the next morning, she had a terrible headache. She took something for it and got dressed. She started to make coffee, but the very thought of it put her off. Eventually her headache eased some, so she gathered the kittens into their traveling cage and headed to work.

By 10:30 that morning, she was coughing and sneezing and sure she was running a temperature. When Merry came in from a call at a farmer's, she took one look at Gina. She was as pale as the paper she typed on and coughing in hard, hacking gasps.

Merry headed to the back where Dan was with a patient. Knocking on the door and sticking in her head, she said, "Do you think that Shirley Browning could come in for a few days? Gina is coming down with the flu. I'm pretty sure she has a fever, and she's having trouble breathing."

Concerned, Dan excused himself and left the client, an elderly lady with a very elderly cat, and followed Merry out to the waiting room. One look at Gina was all it took for him to

88

agree totally with Merry's assessment. "Gina," he said, "as of this moment, you are on sick leave. I'm calling a taxi for you."

"But . . ." said Gina in dismay. If she was away, she'd lose her pay. She'd never been away before and with her tight savings schedule, she was living close to the line. She didn't want to have to start dipping into it.

"No buts," said Merry, putting her hand on Gina's forehead. "You're burning up. Ted can take over the desk until we get a hold of Shirley."

Realizing she didn't have the strength to argue, Gina stood to get her coat. To her utter dismay, the room tilted, and she found herself clinging to the desk for dear life. Merry was around the counter in a flash and steadied her. Then, just when she was sure that life could not get any more complicated, Andy walked in.

Without thinking, she croaked crossly, "What are you doing here?"

Somewhere in the back of her mind where she could still process the odd thought, she had to laugh at his expression. Blank confusion.

Merry piped up, "Good timing, Andy. Gina is sick and needs to go home and to bed. I was just going to call a taxi. Would you be able to take her instead? It would be faster."

Moving closer, Andy could hear that Gina's breathing was labored. Memories of Kelly's frequent infections raised their ugly head. "Call Jim Anderson. Ask if he can see Gina before I take her home. I don't like the way she's breathing."

"Good idea," replied Dan. "I'll give him a ring immediately."

While Andy helped her on with her coat, she could hear Dan's voice from a long way off, as if through some kind of sound tunnel. It seemed to echo. Then she felt the dizziness return and reached out for Andy. With a click of his tongue, Andy swung her up in his arms. "If he won't see her, I'll take her into the hospital in Smithboro."

"Don't want to go to the hospital," she protested.

Andy was swinging toward the door when Dan said, "Doc Anderson will see her right away. He says there is a very nasty flu going around, and he doesn't want her sitting about giving it to anyone else."

From a distance, Gina felt herself floating, as if by magic, into the warm van. Snuggling down into the seat, she began to slide off. "No, you don't," said Andy as he hoisted her up and clicked the seat belt around her.

Jumping into the other side of the van, he fastened his belt and headed for the medical clinic. When they got there, Andy left Gina in the examining room with the doctor and his nurse Helen. He was really worried. He'd never seen anyone quite so sick with the flu. He knew he didn't want to leave her on her own, and he certainly couldn't take her home to his father's place. He was sure that a flu like that could be quite dangerous to his Dad. Then he thought of Cindy. She wasn't tied down to a schedule yet. Maybe she'd come over and help get Gina into bed. He was sure Gina would be furious if he tried to help, although if there was no alternative, he thought grimly, he'd do it anyway.

Using his cell phone, he called Cindy. She said she would come immediately. Hanging up, he wondered if Dan would mind, so he phoned the animal clinic and talked to him.

"I'm glad you thought of Cindy," said Dan. "She had a mild version of that flu just a few weeks before our wedding. Just one thing. Drop back here on the way to Gina's. We'll watch for you. I'm going to send over some masks and plastic gloves. Tell Cindy to wear them."

Andy had just hung up when the doctor came in. "I've just given Gina medication to help her breathing. I'm not very happy about sending her home unsupervised."

"Cindy Hamilton said she'd come over right now and help her get to bed. I think she'll stay for a while."

"Cindy Hamilton?" And then the light dawned. "Oh, you mean the bride. Well, I'm sure Cindy could get her settled. I'm just not happy about Gina spending the night alone until I'm sure the medication is helping. Has she any family around here?"

"As far as I know, she has no family other than an older step-sister in Ottawa. If necessary, I'll stay."

The doctor, remembering Andy's difficult sojourn with Kelly's illness said gently, "Are you sure you want to do that, Andy?"

Andy knew exactly what he was referring to. "I'll stay if I have to," he said gruffly.

"Well, I'm sure you know the routine. Lots of fluids. Try to keep her cooled down. I've already called the pharmacy to get a prescription ready for the cough. You can pick it up on the way over to her place. If she gets worse, leave a message with my answering service and I'll get back to you. Use your judgment. If you think she needs to go to the hospital, call an ambulance."

Andy was really alarmed now. Seeing his expression, the doctor added, "I don't think it will come to that. I'm just covering the usual bases. I'm sure she'll be alright. She's young and healthy."

* * *

Andy put some more wood in the range in Gina's kitchen. Replacing the lid, he turned and looked into the bedroom where Gina was sleeping. She murmured something and tossed an arm out from under the covers, disarranging them. Quietly, he went into the room and straightened them. Then, just to assure himself, he took the thermometer he'd purchased when he picked up the prescription and placed it in her ear. It read her temperature immediately. With a relief, he saw that it was coming down.

Glancing at his watch he saw that it was 11:00. Cindy had stayed until 10:00, helping him get Gina's bed out, get her changed and feed her a clear broth that she had brought with her. It seemed that as a chef, she had a freezer full of such things.

Now he was on his own. Just then he heard a sharp tap on the side door. Going quickly to see who it was, he was surprised to see the doctor. "Come in, Jim. Been up late?"

"Just back from Smithboro. Karen Jackson had twin girls. You should see Dave Jackson. He looks like he personally gave birth to the both of them. Thought I'd just drop in and see how your invalid is. Then, if you were to offer me a cup of tea or coffee, I'd feel human again."

"Sure thing, Jim. Your choice."

"Tea, then."

Andy had just made the tea when the doctor came back into the kitchen. "She's doing nicely. Her temperature has dropped, although it's not back to normal yet. Her lungs seem better too. This flu is a nasty business if you don't look after it. I'm glad she got attention so quickly."

Taking the mug Andy offered, the doctor sat down on a kitchen chair and sipped his tea. Andy offered him some sandwiches Cindy had brought with her.

"Been cooking?"

Andy smiled. "Not me. Cindy. As soon as I told her what was wrong with Gina, she grabbed things from her fridge and freezer and came over. She had the perfect broth for Gina. And I certainly have enjoyed the sandwiches."

The doctor ate his sandwiches and finished his tea before he said anything. Andy was used to Jim Anderson's ways. They'd spent more than one night together during the final days of Kelly's illness.

As if he had read his mind, the doctor said, "Just like old times."

Andy nodded in agreement.

"I don't like to pry, Andy. But am I right in thinking you have a particular interest in that young woman?"

"Yes."

"I'm glad, Andy. I've been concerned about you. I was afraid you were going to withdraw from life completely."

"I think I almost had. For the longest time, I just couldn't see the sense of living without Kelly. We'd been together since our late teens."

Standing, Andy went over and brought the teapot to the table. "I'll always love Kelly. Nothing will change that."

Sitting down again, he turned to the doctor. "But Gina has brought light into my heart again." He smiled at his own words. "I'm not exactly sure where this is all leading. I know I think I could be happy again. Although, sometimes I feel disloyal to Kelly."

The doctor studied him for a few moments but didn't say anything. Finally, Andy said, "Jim. I know your wife died at least ten years ago. How come you haven't married again?"

"Not because I felt guilt, nor should you feel guilt. I think it's probably because of the life I lead. A doctor in a small village isn't really free to date. It is possible to make friends at the hospital, but still the gossip mill is pretty fearsome. And being the only doctor in town doesn't leave much time for socializing."

"Would you like to marry again?"

Andy watched as the long-legged doctor crossed his legs and looked at his foot as if the answer to the question was there. After a few moments, he looked up and smiled at Andy. "Yes, I think I would."

Glancing at his watch, the doctor said, "Well, I'd better get home. I have a heavy day tomorrow. I think Gina is going to be alright now. Are you staying?"

Andy nodded. "Cindy said she'd come back tomorrow morning. I'll snooze on this rocker." He followed the doctor down the hallway and waited while he got his coat. Holding out his hand, he said, "Thanks Jim, for dropping by. I've missed our times together. You're a good friend." Jim took his hand. "Keep in touch."

Andy went back into the kitchen. He looked into the other room where Gina lay sleeping quietly. Going back to the kitchen, he put some more wood into the stove and then, taking an afghan off a chair, wrapped it around his shoulders, turned off all but one small light, and settled into the rocker.

Gina coughed and woke herself up. There was just enough light for her to realize that it must be dawn. She lay there and tried to recall how she got into her bed. And then it all came back: her headache, the speed with which she had become ill, the trip to the doctor and being helped to bed by Cindy. Then she remembered being cradled in Andy's arms, feeling safe in spite of her fever.

For a while, she drifted close to sleep and then she remembered hearing voices sometime through the night. Andy and some other man were talking. Words came back to her. Words she wished she hadn't heard. *I'll always love Kelly. Nothing will change that,* Andy had said. With those words, the small flame of love that Gina had not even realized warmed her heart faltered and went out.

Turning on her side, she buried her face in her pillow and wept.

Andy woke with a jerk when someone knocked at the door. To his surprise, it was daylight. He hunched his shoulders, eased his neck, and wondered how long he'd been asleep. Shrugging off the afghan, he stood and peeked in the room where Gina was still sleeping, then headed for the door.

When he opened it, he discovered Cindy standing there with an armful of parcels. Reaching out to take some, he asked, "What time is it?"

"Eight thirty." Cindy stepped into the hall, wiped her shoes on the hall carpet and hung up her jacket. "How's the patient?"

"Still sleeping, although once through the night, I had to help her along to the washroom. She's still a bit unsteady on her feet. Doc Anderson was here late last night and checked her over. Her breathing has improved and her temperature is coming down."

As Cindy took the parcels from him, she said, "He's a great guy. A real old-time country doctor." Then with a grin, she recalled, "He sure knows what to do when a man faints."

Andy laughed. "I heard all about that. It'll be a wonder if Dan ever lives that little incident down. Fainting at the sight of a needle."

"The needle was going into my arm," Cindy reminded him.

Curious, Andy poked his nose in a paper bag and found some steaming muffins. "Mmmm. Did you make these?"

"Just out of the oven. Made in my new kitchen. Figured you'd be starving." From an insulated bag, she lifted out a coffee pot.

"Is that what I think it is?"

"Sure is. Grab two mugs out of the cupboard."

Moments later, they were both sitting at the kitchen table sipping coffee and biting into muffins. "Dan doesn't know how lucky he is," mumbled Andy with his mouth full.

Cindy grinned. "Oh, I think he does."

Gina was still asleep when they finished. "Look," said Cindy. "Why don't you go home and get some rest. Give me your cell phone number. If there's a problem, I'll let you know. I brought some paperwork I have to do for the tearoom. I'll make sure Gina has lunch. She may be alright on her own after that."

Andy smiled. "Thanks, Cindy. I really appreciate you stepping in. I'll just take a look at Gina before I go."

Andy tiptoed into the sleeping area and walked over to her bed. Gina was sleeping on her side. Her breathing was much quieter than it had been earlier. Tenderly, he reached out and felt her forehead. It seemed cooler too.

Returning to the kitchen, he said, "She's still sleeping. I'm heading home. I'll keep in touch."

Andy had just let himself into the house when his father stuck his head out of the kitchen door. "How's Gina?"

"Quite a bit better. Cindy is with her. I'm going to head off to bed for an hour or so. Carolyn cleared my work load for yesterday and today, so I'll probably hop over to Gina's again later."

His father studied him for a few moments and then said, "I gather Gina means something special to you."

Andy thought about his father's statement for a moment, then said, "I think you might be right." He yawned in spite of himself and then added, "I really didn't expect anything like this to happen to me again. I'm not even sure just how I feel exactly. I just know that being with her makes me happy."

"I'm glad, son. It's good to see you more like your old self. It's important to get on with life. Oh, by the way, I've asked the entire family, Carolyn and David, Naomi and Mike and Ben to come over after supper for an hour. I'd like it if you could be here."

Andy looked at his father in surprise. "What's up?"

"I'd rather talk to you all at once, if you don't mind. I suggested eight o'clock. Another thing, before I forget. I have to go to Smithboro this afternoon. I don't expect to be finished until late, so I'll eat there. Think you can fend for yourself?"

Studying his father carefully, he looked for signs of illness or stress, but nothing seemed to be the matter. "I'll be fine for supper," he said. Still worrying about what his father could possibly want to discuss with the entire family, he headed up the stairs. His father looked good. He was still a handsome man; tall, white-haired, slim since his heart surgery. Maybe it had something to do with the business. It was a good thing he was taking the computer course. He might need it.

Gina woke up coughing again. Moving gingerly, she discovered her headache was gone. Suddenly, she needed the washroom. Carefully, she sat up on the side of the bed. The bathroom was off the hall on the other side of the kitchen.

She was just trying to figure out the safest way to get there when a voice said, "Oh, you're up."

She turned to see Cindy standing in the doorway. "How are you feeling?"

"Much better, although I feel pretty weak."

"Want help getting to the washroom?"

"You're a life saver," said Gina. "I'm not sure I could get there on my own."

Cindy came over and helped her stand up and then let her lean on her until they reached the washroom. "Do you think you can manage in there?"

Gina nodded.

"Good. While you're in there, I'm going to change your bed again. I took your sheets home and washed them in my new washing machine. Call me when you're ready to come back."

When Gina was ready, Cindy helped her down the hall. "Would you like to sit up for a few minutes and try to have something for breakfast?"

Gina nodded. "Although I'm not very hungry."

Cindy got her settled in the rocking chair and then asked, "Tea or coffee or herbal tea?"

Leaning back into the old rocker, another treasure she'd found in the living room, Gina said, "Herbal, I think." Then getting up her courage, she asked, "Did you stay here all night?"

Cindy shook her head. "No. Andy did. Don't you remember? He said he walked you down the hall to the bathroom."

Gina shut her eyes and tried to think. "I remember voices. Andy and someone else."

"Doc Anderson."

Gina opened her eyes at that. "Was I that sick?"

Anxious to assure her, Cindy said, "No. I think he just wanted to be sure. Anyway, I gather he and Andy are old friends. He was very good to Andy when his wife was sick."

And then Gina remembered the words, *I'll always love Kelly. Nothing will change that.* Again she felt an overwhelming sense of loss.

Cindy, watching her, saw the color leave her cheeks. "Are you all right, Gina?"

"Just tired. I'll be better after I've had the tea."

It was true. Gina did feel better. Cindy had made some toast and served it with some delicious honey she'd brought with her. But by the time Gina had finished, she was ready to get into bed.

As Cindy settled her, Gina said, "I don't know how you can be so kind. I was horrible to you last year, trying to interfere with you and Dan."

Cindy sat down on the bed and looked at her. "Listen, Gina. We could make each other sick thinking about what happened last year. But you did the brave thing. You confessed and straightened out everything between Dan and me. Let's bury it right now. I'm glad I was free to help you. You've certainly helped me with things."

"Thanks for forgiving me, Cindy. I will try to bury it. And now, I think I'll probably sleep some more."

Cindy was making soup when there was a knock on the door. Checking the time, she saw that it was close to noon. Glancing in at Gina, she saw that she was still asleep. She hurried to the door only to discover Merry standing there with the cage with the kittens.

As she entered, she said, "I thought the patient could probably use some amusement and these little monkeys are just the ones to entertain."

"Oh, that's a good idea. I think Gina was sort of down after breakfast. She's asleep, but I expect she'll wake very soon. Come in. Have you had lunch? I'm making soup."

"Is that what smells so divine?"

"That and some bread I put in the oven. I had it ready to go at home. Decided this loaf might as well bake here."

Merry peeked in at Gina only to discover that she was sitting at the side of the bed. Taking the cage, she walked in and held it up. "I thought you might be missing your family."

"Oh, thank you." Taking the cage, she set it on the bed and opened the door. In moments, a curious black kitten came out followed by the other two. Gina reached out and picked up the little grey one. "I was just lying in bed wondering where they were."

Cindy came in. "Do you feel well enough to get up and have something to eat? I made some soup."

Still cuddling the kittens, Gina said, "I think so. At least I feel hungry this time. First, I'm off to the bathroom to freshen up."

"Before you do, let's just check your temperature. I see you have one of those fancy thermometers that you poke in your ear. I've always wanted to try one."

Gina frowned at that. "I don't have a thermometer at all. I wonder where that one came from. They're expensive."

"Maybe it belongs to Andy," Merry said as she poked the device in her ear. "You're temperature is much better. You still have a degree above normal but I suspect that by tomorrow it will be back to normal."

"Did you get Shirley to come in?"

"Yes, and you're not to worry. Stay off until you are completely better. And don't worry about your pay. It's looked after."

But by the time the three of them had had soup and played with the kittens, Gina was exhausted. Merry checked her temperature, and it was up a bit. "It's back to bed for you."

She went without argument and was asleep minutes after her head hit the pillow.

As Merry got ready to leave, she asked Cindy, "Is Andy going to come over at supper time? I don't like to think of Gina on her own just yet."

"I think so. I sent him home to get some sleep this morning. I expect he'll be here. I'm going home once I've cleaned up, but I'll get in touch with him to make sure. I'll just give him a little more time to rest. Anyway, he took a key so he can get in."

When Andy woke, he phoned his sister only to discover that she had no idea why her father wanted them all to be at the house that evening. "Do you think he's alright? Has he been to the doctor lately?" asked Carolyn.

"No, he seems perfectly healthy to me. Better than he's been in years. Maybe he wants to retire completely."

"I hadn't thought of that. That's probably it. Thanks, Andy. You've set my mind at rest.

"Oh, by the way," said Carolyn. "I was going to phone you and let you know that David made enough supper for you and Gina. Can you come and pick it up? Are you going to stay there tonight?"

"Yes, to getting supper. I'm not sure about tonight. Thank your dear husband. See you at eight o'clock."

* * *

Andy made it back to his father's house just minutes before 8:00. He had found Gina up and sitting in the rocking chair, the kittens in a bundle on her lap. She was obviously much better, her fever was down and energy level higher. After they'd eaten David's chicken stew, they sat and talked until 7:30. She'd insisted that she was well enough to stay alone and practically pushed him out the door. But something wasn't right. Andy couldn't exactly put his finger on it, but he was uneasy. Not with her health but with her state of mind. Something was bothering her.

When he entered the living room, the family was waiting for their father to present himself. They played the guessing game again; he was going to retire completely, he was going to come back to work because he felt better, he was going to go on a cruise around the world.

At that point, Jim Thompson came in accompanied by Nora. Waiting till she was seated, he said, "I have several important announcements to make." Then he busied himself finding a chair and sitting down beside the housekeeper.

Unable to wait any longer, Carolyn said, "Dad! You've got us all on tender hooks. What is so important that you brought us all in here?" When he didn't answer immediately, she uttered their worst fear. "Are you sick?"

Jim straightened at that. "Do I look sick?"

"Well, no," Carolyn admitted.

"I've asked you here because I want you to be the first to know that Nora and I have decided to get married."

He didn't get a chance to say anymore. His children were all over Nora and himself congratulating them and wanting to know their plans. Finally, he put his hand up and said, "Sit down. I'm not finished."

Mystified, they did as they were told. "I have one more announcement. This may affect you, Andy, more than anyone else since you live here. I've decided to sell the house."

Silence fell as his children and their spouses chewed over this piece of news. The house had been the center of their lives for so many years. And for Andy, it had been the first place he'd come back to after living out in his cabin for so long. Jim watched them.

Andy was the first to speak. "Dad, I have no problem with you selling the house. I'm sure it's too big for you. Where will you and Nora live?"

Jim reached over and put his arm around Nora's shoulder. "We are going to sell both our houses and build a new one. First, we'll sell this one and then stay at Nora's while you guys build the new one we've designed. Then we'll sell hers. We have a lot down by the lake just right for a bungalow. What do you think of that?"

Ben, the plumber in the family, teased, "I think that there has been a lot going on while I've been away from home."

Carolyn said, "I'd love to see the plans so that I can make you a model."

"We were hoping you would," said Nora. Carolyn's models were works of art.

Mike, the oldest and probably the most down to earth said, "You shouldn't have any trouble selling the house. When do you intend to put it on the market?"

Andy thought of Merry and her problems. "I don't think you'll have to put it on the market at all. Dr. Harper is desperate to find a house to buy. This place would be perfect. My apartment would be ideal for Ruth, her housekeeper. Shall I mention it to her?"

"Well, give us a few days," said Jim. "We still have to break the news to Nora's daughter and son."

After that, everyone wanted to see the house plans. Jim and Nora gave in and brought them out.

Glancing at his watch, Andy saw that it was 9:00. He wondered how Gina was. Excusing himself, he headed over to her place.

There were lights on in Gina's house when Andy arrived, so he tapped gently on the door. No answer. Not exactly concerned, he walked around to the back of the house and peeked in the kitchen window. To his relief, he saw Gina in the rocking chair, asleep.

Returning to the side door, he opened it with the key she had given him and tiptoed in. Immediately, he realized that it was quite cool inside. Proceeding to the kitchen, he saw that Gina had changed into a warm track suit and was covered by the same afghan he had used the night before. In her lap were the three kittens, snuggled together for warmth.

"Gina," he whispered but got no response. She appeared to be sleeping deeply. To his relief her breathing was back to normal; in fact, only the rise and fall of her chest suggested that she was breathing at all. Even the kittens were sound asleep, not moving an ear or a whisker when he spoke.

Deciding to deal with the fire first, he carefully opened the top of the stove and, as quietly as he could, popped in several pieces of wood. As he finished, he glanced over to see if she had heard him, but neither she nor the kittens showed any sign of being disturbed.

Unable to stop himself, Andy gave in to the pleasure of

watching Gina sleep. Her head was tipped slightly to the side and in the soft light, her long lashes fanned over softly flushed cheeks. Lush pink lips were slightly open, and he could see the soft glint of ivory. Dark curls, now in disarray, framed her face. She was lovely.

He called her name once more but got no response. Finally, he made a decision. He couldn't leave her in the rocker all night. Going into her bedroom, he straightened the sheets and covers and fluffed up the pillows. Then, returning to the kitchen, he gingerly lifted the kittens off her lap and put them back in their cage. He made sure there was some food and water for them and that they were near enough the stove to keep warm; although he could see that they were stretching and no doubt ready to play.

All the time he fussed with the kittens, Gina slept on. When everything was done, he returned to his problem. Getting Gina to bed. For the third time, he called her, but again, no response. With a sigh, Andy decided there was nothing for it but to lift her up and take her to the bed. He knew he might run the risk of getting his face slapped but he was willing to take the risk. He certainly didn't plan to let her stay in the rocking chair, and there was no need for him to stay the night to watch over her. So, to the bed it was.

Taking a big breath, he reached down and gently lifted her so that her head cradled against his shoulder. He stood and inhaled her sweet scent, then carefully walked into the bedroom. As he approached the bed, she moved slightly and murmured something in her sleep. Unable to help himself, he dropped a kiss on her soft curls and then eased her onto the bed. He covered her carefully and watched her sleep.

Returning to the kitchen, he pulled out a pencil and small notepad from his shirt pocket and wrote, *Gina, You fell asleep in the rocking chair. I couldn't wake you, so I tucked you into bed. I also fed the kittens and put wood on the fire. See you tomorrow afternoon. I'm picking up the electrical panel in the morning and can begin to install it after lunch. If you have any problem through the night, phone me.* He left his number and signed his name.

One last glance told him that she was still in a dead sleep; sleep she no doubt needed now that the worst of the flu was over. Locking the door behind him, he left for his dad's place, ready for a full night's sleep himself, but not before he notified Carolyn that he intended to work at Gina's in the afternoon.

When Andy came down the next morning he found his father sitting at the kitchen table, a mug of coffee in his hand, the newspaper propped up in front of him. When Andy had sat down with a mug also, he said, "How was Gina last night?"

"Out like a light."

"You didn't think she needed someone with her?"

Andy smiled. "No, Dad, I didn't. Her temperature was back to normal, her color good and breathing as it should be. I expect, though, that this morning she'll be a little annoyed with me. When I came in, she was sound asleep in the rocking chair. Although she had an afghan over her, the house was cold, and I figured that if she stayed there, she'd end up with a stiff neck. So I tucked her in."

Finishing his coffee, Andy got up and started to make himself some breakfast. As he worked, his father said, "I've been thinking about Merry and this house. I understand she registered with Art Cramer. He's spent time showing her one or two places. I think, to be fair, we should get Art in. He can give us an assessment. We can get another one if we think his is off. Let's face it, anyone in this family has a pretty good notion about the value of the property. Anyway, I'm sure Art's assessment will be accurate."

Andy thought about this for a moment. "I suspect you're right. I think Merry is bound for ninety days to deal with him but maybe I'm wrong. I'll check."

He broke two eggs into water and slipped toast into the toaster. While he waited for them to be ready, he turned and asked his father, "How long did all of you talk last night?"

His father got a downright silly grin on his face. "Until almost eleven o'clock. Nora and I had to go over all our plans. We also talked about things each of you would like out of this house. There is enough furniture to fill several. And we set a date."

Andy raised his eyebrow at this. "Fast work, Dad," he teased. "When?"

"The long weekend in April. On the Saturday."

"Wow. You really do work fast. That's less than a month from now."

"Well, I'm counting on you all giving us a hand."

Andy served up his breakfast and sat down. "Merry has to be out of Cindy's parent's place by the first of May."

"Well, that would work out. We could make the closing date the Saturday before the wedding. I can stay with Caroline until the wedding. I'm going to phone Art this morning. I'll see what he thinks. Don't say anything to Merry if you see her. Let Art do the talking."

"Sure, Dad. I'm finished over at the clinic anyway. I'm going to pick up the materials for Gina's new electrical service. I've a small job to do for Carolyn this morning and after lunch, I'm going to start work at Gina's."

"I didn't think she'd let you start that until she had funds."

"Didn't I tell you? We're doing a trade. I'm getting computer lessons. Gina is getting new wiring."

Jim laughed. "You're a crafty one, son."

The coolness of the house finally woke Gina. Opening her eyes, she was astonished to see that it was broad daylight. How long had she slept? Glancing at her watch, she saw that it was 10:00. For a moment, she panicked. She was late for work. But then a fit of coughing reminded her that she was sick. Or had been sick, she thought. She felt much better at that moment.

The sound of mewing had her sitting up on the side bed. She was relieved to discover that she was no longer dizzy. Then she realized that she'd gone to bed in her tracksuit. She frowned for a moment, trying to make sense of that.

The kittens must have heard her for they started crying all the louder. "Okay, little guys," she called. "I'm coming."

Still frowning, she looked down for her slippers. There they were set primly a foot or so down the side of the bed. She never left her slippers there. She never left her slippers neatly placed anywhere. She frequently had to rescue one from under the bed. Then the truth dawned. Someone had put her to bed.

She had been sitting in the rocker enjoying the heat of the fire and the warmth of the kittens in her lap. She'd intended to watch her small TV but couldn't remember even doing that. She must have fallen asleep.

Standing, she stepped into the errant slippers and headed for the kitchen. On the table, she spotted a piece of note paper propped against a mug. Picking it up, she read it. She blinked and read it again. Andy Thompson had put her to bed! And she couldn't even remember it!

Suddenly, she was embarrassed. Not because he'd carried her to bed, covered her up, and no doubt left her to snore herself silly, but because she was sure she was anything but daisy fresh. When had she last washed her hair or cleaned her teeth? Yuck.

She reread the note. He was coming here? After lunch? She glanced at the clock over the kitchen sink. It was 10:10 now.

Again the cries of her charges reminded her that they were probably famished. Hurrying to the cupboard, she got out their food and a fresh dish of water. Although they were able to come out of the cage and skitter around the kitchen, she decided to leave them in it while she had a shower.

She put wood on coals that were barely glowing, grabbed fresh clothing and hurried into the bathroom to make herself decent. It was only as she was blow-drying her hair that she remembered the words she had heard when she was so sick. *I'll always love Kelly.* She stopped brushing her hair and looked at her reflection in the mirror. Then why, she asked herself, was Andy taking such good care of her; staying with her when her fever was high, checking on her to see if she was safe, putting her to bed and now, coming to work on her house? Her reflection did not answer her.

Chapter Seven

Andy stepped into the small restaurant on Main Street to have lunch. The house specialty was English-style fish and chips. The slight tang of salt and vinegar wafting from the plates of two teenage boys made him give up on the idea of a health conscious lunch. He was hungry.

Looking around, he saw that there was still a small table at the back. As he headed for it, he noticed the guy who'd left the cats sitting at the table next to it. He was drinking a coffee and studying a book.

Curious, Andy settled in his chair and then said, "Hi. It's Nick, isn't it?"

Andy had obviously interrupted him, because Nick looked at him for a moment before he seemed to recognize him.

"Oh, hi. Andy. Sorry. I didn't see you."

At that moment, the waitress came and took Andy's order. She also filled Nick's mug again. When she left, Andy asked, "What are you studying?"

Nick blushed and held up a textbook. "Wiring."

110

Andy was intrigued. "That's not what you're studying at night, is it?"

"No," said Nick. "I need my grade twelve credits to get into the apprenticeship course. I had to leave school at the end of grade eleven because my Dad died. For the past few years, I've been working at any job I could get my hands on until my younger sister finished school. My mom has just married again, so I'm free now to see if I can qualify."

When Andy's food came, they continued to chat while he ate. Andy learned that Nick had actually helped a handyman do a lot of small electrical jobs and had picked up quite a few tricks of the trade. When Andy had finished his meal, Nick packed up his books. "I'm off to the library now to do some reading. I'm working on an English credit. See you around."

Andy was impressed. Nick seemed to have a good grasp of the material in the book he was reading. He'd keep an eye on him. They were always looking for hardworking people for the business. Come to think of it, Tim, his apprentice, was going to write his final exams in June. Maybe Nick would make a good candidate for a new apprentice. It might be worth asking them to give him a hand with a few small jobs. He'd mention it to his Dad.

Merry stepped into the reception area with a prescription for Maestro, a lovely large Persian famous for his eloquent meows, especially when he was transported in a carrier. Going over to where his owner was closing the door of his carrier, she said, "Here are the antibiotics for Maestro, Mrs. Jarvos. Do you remember how to give the pills to him?"

"Oh yes," she said, "It's always a battle of wills. Maestro can keep his jaw clamped shut when it suits him. Fortunately for me, he has a liking for butter. The pill is down his throat before he knows what he's swallowed."

Merry laughed. "Thank goodness for a little honest greed. It makes our job easier."

Just then, the temporary receptionist interrupted. "Dr. Harper. I have a call from Art Cramer for you."

Merry hurried around to take the phone. Maybe Art had something new on the market. Saying a silent prayer, she said, "Hello Art."

She listened carefully, glanced at her watch, and then said, "Sure Art. How about three o'clock if you can arrange it? If you come over here, I'll follow you to the house."

Merry put the phone down and danced a little jig just as Dan came through the door. "Good news?" he asked.

"Maybe. Art was a little cagey. He thinks he's found the perfect house. But until I see it, he wants to keep the address secret. The owner hasn't put a sign up yet. Can you cover for me at three? Right now, my list is finished at two-forty-five."

"Sure thing. Good luck. Let me know how it goes."

Gina felt cranky and out of sorts. By the time she'd made breakfast, she was exhausted. To make matters worse, she spent a great deal of time coughing. Now, it was 1:15. All she wanted to do was go to sleep, but she couldn't. Andrew Thompson was supposed to be coming. He said he'd be there right after lunch, but he was late. That fact irritated her unreasonably. Angry at herself for being so miserable, she flopped in the rocker, intent on trying to soothe herself when she heard him knock at the door.

Heaving a sigh, Gina went to the door, scowling with the effort to control her bad temper. She opened it to discover Andy standing there with an armful of material and a tall lanky young man standing directly behind him with a coil of wire over his shoulder.

Stepping back, Gina let them in. The young guy grinned at her happily. *Oh great,* she thought, *two of them to deal with.*

Andy said, "Gina, I'd like you to meet my apprentice, Tim."

Unable to find the energy to give a perky response, she said, "Hi, Tim," and turned to head down the hall.

She heard Andy tell Tim where to put the wire as she headed for the rocker. Suddenly, she didn't think she'd make it. *Darn flu,* she groused.

Andy looked after her in surprise. His first impression had been that Gina was feeling a lot better. She was dressed and had obviously washed and dried her hair. But the silent retreat down the hall sent a warning he couldn't miss. Deciding to get the rest of the supplies in before bothering her, he set Tim to work bringing in his tools and headed to the small room opposite the bathroom where the ancient washer and dryer took about half the space.

When Carolyn and he had examined the house for the grant, he'd picked a place for the power box. Now, he checked the spot, looked for studs on which to fasten the box, and checked to see whether there was adequate room to run the power lines where he wanted them. When he'd done all he could, he headed for the kitchen.

Gina's eyes fluttered open when he came in. He noted her pallor. She wasn't quite as perky as she must have been when she woke up. Thinking of her waking up, he wondered if her briskness at the door had been annoyance.

"Gina," he said softly. "I need to disturb you for a moment. I want to see if the spot I've chosen for the power box suits you."

He could tell she was subduing a sigh when she stood up and headed down the hall. Andy realized she wasn't feeling all that well. He'd had enough experience with Kelly's illness to recognize the signs of someone trying hard to manage a civil tongue when all they wanted to do was sleep. However, she listened carefully while he explained his choice for the location of the box and stood obediently before the wall so he could figure out just how high he would place it. He wanted her to be able to reach the top switches.

Thanking her carefully, he left her to wander back down the hall.

Tim and he worked for about two hours before he went back to check on her. He was just in time to see her stand and yawn. This time her color was back to normal. When she saw him, she gave him a tentative smile.

"Feeling better?" he asked.

"Much better than before. I'm sorry. When you came I was just wiped."

"You know, Tim and I could use a tea or coffee. Would you like me to make a pot?"

He could see that she was ready to insist that it was her house, when a hungry meow interrupted her. He was amused to watch her struggle with her priorities. Finally she said, "That would be great if you would. I think tea would be best. Right now, I don't even think I want to smell coffee. I'll feed the kittens."

He made the tea and found mugs while she put out fresh dishes of food and water and placed them on a mat near the stove. Then she let the animals out. They both watched with amusement while the three young creatures made for the food, shoving and pushing when they reached the dish and managing to step into the water in their effort to get their share.

"Greedy wee beasts," Gina said.

"Aren't they just?" he agreed.

Bringing her attention back to the tea, Gina said, "There are some cookies in that cupboard at the end. Maybe you would put them out on a plate."

Andy was just about to say that he didn't expect her to feed them when she said firmly, "If you intend to work on my house, I reserve the right to give you coffee or tea breaks and supply cookies."

He had enough sense to bow to her decision.

When Art Kramer arrived at the clinic, he gave Merry more details about the house. "The owner has just decided to get married again. His children are grown and have all left home except one son who only stayed at the house to be around while his father was recovering from heart surgery."

"It was a family home, then?" Merry asked.

"Yes. I suspect you've met some of the family. It's Jim Thompson's house."

Merry couldn't keep down the surge of hope at his words. "Jim Thompson, the father of Andy Thompson?"

"That's the man."

"Why that's a wonderful house. When did it come on the market?"

"Jim was in to see me today. He suggested I contact you. It seems his children all know you're looking for a place. If it suits you and you two can agree on a suitable price, I think Jim will be happy to sell it to you. Mind you, you won't have a chance to haggle like you might if we put it on the market."

Bidding Art good-bye, Merry got in her car and sat looking at the Thompson house. It was vintage Victorian with ginger-bread trim and a tower. As Art had said on the way over, there wasn't a house in Stewart's Falls in better condition. Jim Thompson and his brood were famous for the quality of their work and that was evident when she went through the house.

It was everything she dreamed of and so much more. There was a fine apartment on the third floor that would easily accommodate Ruth and her son. Beside the master suite with its ensuite bathroom, there was a spacious room for Michael. It was the *so much more* that worried her. The house had two other bedrooms, two more bathrooms, a lovely staircase, study and a gracious living and dining room. The kitchen was every woman's dream. In the basement, there was a family room made for romping about, perfect for two little boys.

Merry started the car up and headed for Gina's. She wanted to check and see if there was anything she could do for her. As she drove along, Merry continued to think about the house. It had the perfect back yard, fenced and treed, and a great work shed and garage. There was absolutely nothing wrong with the house except that it was so big. The Thompsons had raised four kids in that house. Between Ruth and herself, there were just two boys and no doubt, when the boys got bigger, Ruth would want to move on. In her own present marital situation, there was no chance of there being any more children. She must be crazy to be even thinking of buying the house.

When Merry reached Gina's house, she saw Andy's truck. That made her smile. She had to give Andy a lot of credit. He must be really interested in Gina. He sure seemed to be giving it his best shot.

Andy answered the door when she knocked. "Hi Merry. Gina's in the kitchen. Go right through."

Merry was dying to talk about the house with Andy but Gina's needs came first, so she hurried into the kitchen. She found Gina tucked into the rocker, the orange kitten on her lap as she watched TV.

"Hi, Gina. How are you today?"

Gina started to struggle to get up, but the blanket on her knees seemed to have a life of its own and wouldn't come free when she jerked on it. Merry thought she heard her mutter, "I told him I didn't need to be tucked in."

Just as the blanket loosened, Merry said, "Stay where you are. The kitten is too comfortable to disturb."

Distracted by mention of the kitten, Gina stroked its tiny head. "She's a sweetheart, isn't she?"

Nodding, Merry asked again, "How are you feeling?"

"I'm just fine. Feeling better by the moment," and then she started coughing. Merry waited and then handed her a tissue.

"I'm fine, really," said Gina just as Andy came into the kitchen. "I think I'll be able to go back to work on Monday morning."

"Not unless Doc Anderson says you can," said Andy.

Merry watched with interest while Gina's face pinked up with temper and her eyes sparked. Merry was glad she was to one side of the room so she wouldn't be struck dead by the look Gina gave Andy.

To change the subject, Merry said, "I was just over to look at your father's house, Andy."

Andy raised his eyebrows at this. "Art sure works fast."

"I think your father practically twisted his arm to get Art to phone me."

Gina looked confused and was obviously trying to make sense of the conversation. Andy explained. "My father and

Nora have decided to get married and move into Nora's place until they can build a new house. Dad wants to sell the house. We thought it might be the perfect place for Merry."

"But where will you live if the house is sold?" asked Gina.

"I'll go back to my place out on the lake. I only came into town to be with Dad while he recovered from his surgery."

Turning to Merry, Andy asked, "What did you think of the house?"

Merry looked troubled when she said, "It's a wonderful house. I don't suppose there's a nicer house in the village."

"But? Too expensive?" asked Andy.

"No," said Merry. "I could comfortably carry the house. It's just that it's so big. I don't know how I'd keep up with the housework. And there are rooms we'd never use."

Andy held up his hand. "Don't write off the need for more rooms. Life has a funny way of serving up surprises. Just when you think the important things are over, new things happen."

Gina frowned at this statement, finding it far too philosophical for her present state of mind. Merry got the message and thought that Andy was truly smitten.

Suddenly, Gina piped up, "Merry, couldn't you have someone come in and do the heavy cleaning?"

For some reason, Merry hadn't thought of that.

Andy asked, "Doesn't Ruth do housework for you?"

"Yes," said Merry. "But her real job is to care for the two boys. She insists on doing the housework too, but I can't see her doing that in your father's house. It's far too big. But maybe, as Gina suggested, I could get someone to do the heavy work." Turning to Andy, she said, "I really do love the house. Your family has made it into such a wonderful home that even empty, I'm sure it would welcome us."

Merry stood up. "Gina, I'm going over to the grocers. Are there things I could pick up for you?"

"Actually, that would be a great help. I'll make you a list." Finally making it out of the rocking chair with only a slight frown in Andy's direction, she headed to her tiny telephone desk and started to write a list.

As Gina wrote, Merry said, "I can pick up one of those little barbecue chickens for you. That will give you more than one meal. My treat."

When Gina looked as if she wanted to object, "Let me spoil you. We miss you at the clinic. Take it easy and rest until next week. When Dr. Anderson says you're okay, let us know."

Oblivious to the cross look Gina sent Andy at the mention of the word *doctor*, Merry picked up her purse and sailed out.

Later, Andy was heading for the hall when Gina said, "Andrew Thompson. Dr. Anderson didn't say anything about having to see him when I was in his office. Quit trying to run my life."

Andy said over his shoulder, "Jim was here later that night. Remember? He came to check on you. I'm sure he said he wanted to see you."

The mention of the other night brought back the words that haunted Gina. They made her suspicious of Andy's motivation. Why was he here fussing over her safety? It didn't make sense when he'd said that he'd always love his first wife.

She called after him as she heard him start to gather up his tools. "I'll go back to work when I think I'm ready."

Andy turned on his drill and drilled an imaginary screw

into the wall. Better she think he didn't hear her. He knew enough not to argue with a recuperating patient. Maybe he had gone a little bit overboard with Gina about seeing the doctor. Jim Anderson had said no such thing about wanting to see her.

Andy closed his tool box and sat back on his heels to think. Why had he made up that story? The answer was clear, of course. He was slipping into habits he'd developed with Kelly. It had taken him a long time at the beginning of her illness to realize that she had to call the shots as long as she could.

Going back into the kitchen, Andy said, "Gina. I apologize for interfering. Go back to work when you want. It was stupid of me to tell you what to do. I just got carried away. I really would be very upset if something happened to you."

Gina started to get down the kittens' food. With her back to him, she felt able to ask him a question that was troubling her. "How do you feel about your father remarrying?"

Something about the way Gina was standing, holding the can of cat food, caught his attention. This question was important. "I'm glad for Dad. Mom died a long time ago. Carolyn was only fifteen years old."

"But . . ." she didn't know how to ask what she wanted to know. "Did you ever think he would love someone else as he loved your mother?"

"That's not how it works, Gina. He will never love Nora like he loved my mother. On the other hand, he would never love my mother as he loves Nora now. They are two different people living in two different times."

She continued to fiddle with the cat food, hunting for a can opener and snapping the device on the can and beginning to turn the handle. Andy watched her for a moment or so. For some reason, she was still worrying.

"You know, Gina," he said gently, "I will always love Kelly. What we had was rich and wonderful. But I've discovered that it is possible to move on, to keep that memory in my mind but to live in the present and to try to build a new life."

He went over to her and took the can opener and can from her. "Stupid thing must be dull," she muttered.

As he quickly and efficiently removed the lid on the can he asked, "Do you understand what I'm trying to say?"

"I suppose so," she said still looking at the can of food.

Taking a chance, Andy tipped her head up with a finger so that she had to look at him. "What I'm saying is that I'm ready to love again just as my father is."

With that, he hurried back to his toolbox. When she finally made her way down the hall, he said, "If you think you can stand having me around tomorrow, I'd like to work on this. Next week I have a lot of work lined up. I promise not to get in your way or to get too bossy."

At that, she gave him a sweet smile, and his heart did a ridiculous dance in his chest. "I think I should be feeling much better tomorrow."

Just then, they heard a knock at the door and Merry stuck in her head. "Got your groceries here." Andy reached out and took the bags. "I've got to go now. I promised I'd check in at the clinic before I go home. See you Monday, Gina."

When he returned from placing the food in the kitchen, he said. "I've got to go too. I promised my dad that I'd give him a hand going over all the things he needs to do before the wedding."

Gina stood at the door and watched Andy and Tim drive away. Suddenly, the place seemed empty. Then the smell of the chicken reached her. For the first time in several days, she felt really hungry. As she prepared her supper, she mulled over what Andy had said. He was ready to love again. He said it to her. Looked her right in the eye when he said it. If that was the case, just how did she feel? Was she just attracted because he was good-looking and kind? Was this infatuation? She certainly didn't know whether she was in love. She wished she had someone to talk to about it. But who?

Merry worked at her embroidery and listened for Ruth. She'd asked her to come down once she had her son tucked in for the night. She needed to talk to Ruth before she made her decision about the house.

Ruth came down the stairs quietly. "They're both asleep."

Merry got up and brought in a tray with cocoa. "Sit down, Ruth. I have a problem and I'd like to discuss it with you."

When they were settled, Merry said, "You know, of course, that I've been looking for a house. Also, you know that we can't stay here after June first."

Ruth nodded her head and took a sip of her cocoa.

Merry continued. "I saw a super house today."

"That's wonderful," said Ruth.

"However, there's a problem."

If Merry hadn't been so focused on what she was going to say, she would have noted that Ruth's hands trembled slightly, and she put down her cocoa on a nearby coffee table.

"Do you know the Thompson house? It's the big grey Victorian place with the tower."

"Yes. I know it. My husband played with the youngest son, Ben. He's the one that's a plumber." Ruth paused for a moment and seemed to search for the right words. Finally, she said, "What is the problem?"

"It's too big. It's got an apartment on the third floor and four bedrooms, numerous bathrooms and even a large family room in the basement. It would suit a family of six or seven."

Ruth listened but didn't respond.

"Here's the real problem, Ruth. The house is too big even for the both of us."

Again, Merry missed the way Ruth bit her lip at these words. "There is no way that you could look after it and the boys. Would you mind if I got extra help in? Just to do the heavy work? That would give you time to care for the boys and to cook just as you do now. On the weekends, when I'm free, then you'd have your weekend free just as you have it now. Only, you'd really have your own apartment. You could have your own friends in and even have your mother stay overnight if she was well enough."

"You mean you were worried about my minding someone else cleaning?"

Merry nodded.

"Oh, Merry, I thought you were going to tell me that you wouldn't need me when you got this new house." To Merry's amazement, tears began to trickle down Ruth's face. "I was afraid you wouldn't be able to find a place that was big enough for Pete and myself."

Instantly, Merry was on her feet and over to where Ruth sat, wiping her tears with her fingers. "Oh, Ruth. I never imagined you would think I would leave you behind. This arrangement works so well for us. I did see one small rental house that Mike and I could have managed in, but I didn't want to go there without you." She handed Ruth a tissue and waited until she had herself under control.

"You don't know what a relief it is to know that you want

us," said Ruth. "And I think it would be a very good idea to have someone come in to do the housecleaning. I can manage meals and the boys. I can also pick up and keep things tidy."

"Well, then," said Merry with a grin, "Tomorrow we'll take the two boys over to see the Thompson house. Jim said it would be okay. He would like the matter settled as soon as possible."

The next morning, Gina was surprised to see another man with Andy when she opened the door. After a moment, she realized that she knew his face. She'd seen him around the library on the evenings she taught her course.

She stood back to let them in. As soon as Andy put down his tool box, he said, "Gina, I'd like you to meet Nick Mitchell. He's going to give me a hand today. I hope that's alright."

It wasn't exactly. Gina had thought about what Andy had said the day before and had decided to discover whether what she felt for Andy was really love. She hadn't any particular plan to follow, but she'd thought that if she spent some time with him, she might begin to have a clue about her true feelings. However, the young man beside Andy was watching anxiously, as if his life depended on her agreement, so she scrapped that plan.

"Sure," she said. "When would you like coffee?"

"Probably in an hour. By the way, how are you feeling today?"

"Much better." She spun around. "Don't I look it?"

Andy looked at her for an unnerving moment. Did she have a zit on her chin? "You've got a smudge of lipstick here," he said and reached over and touched her lip. She jumped. Did he have lightning in his fingertips? She felt his touch all the way down to her toes.

Hastily, she turned and headed back to the kitchen, her fingers touching her lip. When she reached it, she leaned against the counter and tried to calm herself. If his fingertip made her toes curl, what would a kiss do? Suddenly, she had an urgent need to know.

She felt a surge of energy that had her deciding she would make cookies. Maybe that would impress him. That thought made her pause. Was that what she was about? Wanting to impress? She thought about her impulse for a moment. No, that wasn't what she wanted to do. She wanted to please him.

An hour to the minute later, she wandered down the hall. She found both men busily working a thick electrical wire up through the box they'd installed in the wall. Nick was hunched down, working the wire up from a roll while Andy was guiding it through a slot in the center of the metal panel. As he worked, Gina watched with fascination as the muscles moved beneath his t-shirt. He'd stripped off the sweat shirt he arrived in and now his arms were bare to above the elbow. Again she found herself intrigued. She surprised herself by discovering she wanted to touch his arm. Maybe run her hand down his back over those moving muscles.

Was this love or just attraction? This desire to touch. She'd never had the urge to touch Dan, although she had liked to hold on to him. She realized that had been a sign of her own insecurity. She'd always felt that if she didn't have a hand on Dan, he might just slip away. And, of course, he had.

As she listened, she realized that Andy was questioning Nick and listening carefully to his answers. He was also explaining everything they were doing.

Some movement from her must have alerted Andy to her

presence, for he turned and asked, "Have you come to tell us what that wonderful smell is?"

So he liked the smell of her cookies. "Come and see. You can freshen up in the bathroom," she said and hurried back to the kitchen.

Rubbing his hands together, Andy hurried into the kitchen and right to the cookie plate. "Mmmm. Chocolate chip cookies. How did you guess my favorite?"

Very pleased with this reaction, Gina replied, "I know they're popular with the staff at the clinic. I also know that your sister is always making them. It was a reasonable guess."

The three of them settled around her kitchen table. "Help yourself," Gina said and watched Andy wolf down three with his coffee. Nick, to her surprise, took one and nibbled on it cautiously.

"Don't you like them, Nick?" she asked. Then she wished she hadn't, because he turned bright red.

"I love them. I just didn't want to appear greedy."

Gina held up the plate and insisted he take several more. Then she turned to Andy. "Do you think Merry will buy your father's house?"

"I really don't know. I expect she needs time to think about it. Dad's willing to give her several days to decide before putting it on the market. He's also said she could come over with the boys and Ruth this morning to check it out."

When the plate was empty, the two men thanked her and returned to work. Gina cleaned up, happy that her cookies had been a hit.

Jim Thompson knew Ruth and welcomed her and the two boys warmly. When Merry asked him to accompany her so she could ask questions, he agreed.

They started in the living room. Merry stood there and tried to imagine her sofa and chairs in the space. They would be perfect. Even the walls would complement the color. Of course, she could always change it later if she wanted to. The boys were enthusiastic about the family room in the basement. Michael was anxious to see where he might sleep if they got the house. When Merry showed him the bedroom she thought he might like, he asked if he could have bunk beds. That's if they bought the house.

But it was when they entered the apartment on the third floor that Merry knew for sure that she was going to buy the house. Ruth was unable to keep the wistful expression off her face. There was a good-sized bedroom that Merry noted was neat and tidy. Next door, there was a room with a desk and a computer. The room would make a very nice room for Peter.

Merry watched Ruth carefully as she asked, "What do you think of this apartment?"

Ruth was not quite able to keep the hope out of her voice when she said carefully. "It's a super place. Imagine, the living room has part of the tower just like the rooms below. One could make window seats and sit there and watch the world go by."

"You think you could keep up with everything?"

"I'd try."

"Then, let's go and see Jim Thompson. Maybe you could take the kids for a walk up to the dairy bar on the main street while I talk over terms. I won't be long."

Merry smiled as she watched Ruth steer the boys out the door and down the stairs with promises of ice cream. Ruth's happiness eased something in Merry's heart that she hadn't realized was there; some tightness that had sat around her heart ever since her husband died. It was as if she suddenly had rediscovered the joy of others' pleasure.

Andy left Nick to pack up and went into the kitchen to see how Gina was doing. He was surprised to see her sitting at the table with a note pad, a textbook, and a three-ring binder. As he watched, she stifled a yawn and then closed the textbook. She realized she was being watched and tried to swallow another yawn.

Andy laughed. "I guess this means you're really feeling better, even if you are yawning."

"You weren't supposed to see that," she said as she stood and picked up the books. "I'll have you know that I've got everything ready for Tuesday's lessons." Then she looked worried. "When are we going to make up for your lessons I've missed this week?"

"Well, not Monday. I have to try to finish a job I started earlier this week. How about Wednesday after work?"

She nodded and then yawned again in spite of herself. "How is the work coming in the laundry room?"

"We've get the panel mounted and some wires threaded into it. Now, the hard part begins. We have to fish the wires up through the walls to the attic."

"Like fishing?" she asked.

"Yeah. It's sort of like that. Especially when the insulation in this house is bark and newspapers and anything else the original owners could find to stuff into it. I'm afraid we'll have to make the odd hole in the wall. I'll try to repair any damage to the wall when we finish."

Andy heard Nick beginning to take the tools outside. "Before I go, I wondered if you'd like to drive out to see my home on the lake tomorrow. I'm going to start transferring my things back there so the apartment can be cleaned before Merry gets the house. That's if she buys it."

When Gina seemed to fidget rather than give him an answer, he added, "The weather promises to be good. The trip will give you a chance to see just how you feel. You'll know better whether you're ready to go back to work."

"I'm going back to work on Monday, regardless of how I feel," she declared stubbornly.

Andy had to hide his admiration for her determination to go back to the clinic. "I'm sure you will. Come tomorrow. I'll bring a picnic and we can eat in the living room and watch the birds."

"What birds?" she asked. "Surely you don't have a feeder out there? How would you keep it full of seeds?"

"Come and find out. I'll pick you up between ten-thirty and eleven. Wrap up so we can also go for a walk. You'll like it out there. It's beautiful."

He wasn't sure why she was finding it so hard to say yes. He could tell she really wanted to go. Sure that she was probably feeling guilty that he had spent time with her when she was sick, he gave her a reason for coming. "You can give me a hand putting some of my things back in place."

She smiled at that. "Okay. I'd like to come."

"Ten-thirty tomorrow morning," Andy said and headed down the hall before she could change her mind.

Chapter Eight

As he pulled into Gina's place, Andy thought that the day couldn't be more perfect. It was unseasonably warm. Almost seventy degrees. There always seemed to be scarce days during this season when the temperature soared, people ran around in their shorts, and frantically looked for the suntan lotion. This warm weather was always short-lived.

Getting out of the van, he stopped to admire crocus and grape hyacinths that grew along the side of the house. A fat robin hopped across the lawn. Andy's spirits soared. Today was going to be a good day. He just knew it.

Gina was ready when he knocked. As he had suggested, she had dressed warmly in jeans, a blouse, soft blue sweater, and a light green jacket. She'd also had the sense to wear hikers.

"Perfect," he said, looking her over and was amused to see her blush.

She showed him a bag. "I brought some things. Suntan lotion if we walk and runners for inside when we work." Then with a glint of mischief in her eyes, she added, "I also brought some shorts just in case it's warm enough to sit in the sun."

Andy couldn't argue with that. The thought of Gina in shorts was far too delightful.

Andy's place was about twenty-five minutes outside Stewart's Falls on a lake that was part of a series of lakes flowing across southeastern Ontario and finally draining into Lake Ontario.

As they drove along, Gina couldn't help but remark, "I was really only sick for three days. I can't believe how the trees have changed in that time. It's as if an artist took a brush and washed pinks, greens, and yellows all over the branches. Everything seems to be coming to life." Pointing to the willows growing along the ditches, she enthused, "Look at the color of those bushes. Their stems are a lovely, rich red."

Andy watched and listened. Gina was like a different person today. Her color had returned. She glowed with enthusiasm. His heart lifted and his determination strengthened. He knew now that he loved her. He wanted to win her heart.

They turned off the country road and headed in through the bush, around large granite outcroppings and past gurgling streams. Finally they turned down toward his place.

When Gina stepped out of the van, she stood and took a deep breath. "Smell the earth. It's wonderful." Then, turning toward the lake, she exclaimed, "The ice is still in."

Andy took her hand and said, "Come with me." He felt her hesitate for a moment, her hand tensing, and then it relaxed in his grip.

He led her down the path to the edge of the lake. Along the shoreline there was a small beach and then a shelf of granite that rose up and then flattened to make a small plateau. "We come out here in the summer and sun ourselves." Still holding her hand, he helped her up onto it.

A sudden movement caught Gina's eye. "Oh, look. There's a bird going down the side of the tree."

"A nuthatch," said Andy. "Haven't you seen any in your backyard?"

Gina pulled a face. "I'm a city girl, Andy. The only birds I know are blue jays and robins."

They stood and looked out over the sullen ice, grey against the pastels of the trees, the dark greens of the pines, and the blue of the sky. A haunting moan shivered its way across the lake. "What on earth was that?" asked Gina.

"It's the ice moving. Look across the lake. Can you see that it's darker on the other side" Gina nodded. "That's where the main current runs. And look to the right there, just before the lake disappears from view. Can you see that you're looking at water there?"

Gina squinted against the sunshine. "You're right. I do see it."

"That means that the ice could go out any time. It just needs a good wind to help it. Possibly the current will be enough to pull the ice out of the bay."

Gina's eyes danced with excitement. "Do you really think so? Today?"

Helping her down off the granite, Andy said, "I really couldn't guess. I've seen it sit like that for days and then disappear over night. Sometimes it goes out and comes right back in. My neighbors always have bets going as to what day it will finally disappear."

They walked along the shore for a few moments. Between the land and ice, a small band of water reflected a tree.

"Look," said Gina. "The image's perfect." At that moment, a duck coasted in and landed on the water, sending ripples of light in its wake.

They both stood, spellbound, as the little fowl dipped and dived in the waves, completely ignoring their presence. "What is it?" Gina whispered.

"A hooded merganser. We're lucky we're far enough away to see him land. Any closer and he would have gone somewhere else."

For a while they watched the little creature diving and surfacing. Finally, Andy said, "Come along. You haven't seen the cottage yet."

Again he took her hand. They walked along the shore past a stand of tall cedars that hid the cottage from view. "Shut your eyes," he said. When she did, he led her around the cedars to where a building stood, built back into the hill about forty feet from the water. Across the front of the old log building a screened verandah stretched. In front of that, there was a wooden deck.

"You can look now."

Gina opened her eyes. She didn't know exactly what she'd expected but it wasn't this. He'd said a house and she'd imagined a modern home. And then he'd mentioned the word cottage and she'd imagined a small building. But this was a large log structure. Its walls had a seasoned look that suggested a good age. It had two stories and a heavily slanted roof and dormer. On the side she could see there was a large window on each floor. It was framed by tall pines and maples.

"It's lovely, Andy," she said. "I didn't realize it was a real log cabin. I've never been in one."

"Actually, it's an old lodge. People used to come up here

to fish and hunt." He led her to the deck, unlocked the veran-dah door, and led her across it to the main entrance.

Gina was charmed. Wooden furniture and a swing filled the space. "It must be wonderful out here in the summer evenings.

"It's really great. You can sit here in the spring and watch the ducks without being eaten alive by mosquitoes." Point-ing at the furniture, he added, "I had cushions made for the chairs and swing." Unlocking the door, he gestured that she should go in first. "Welcome to my home."

The room she entered was large with a staircase going up the back wall to the second floor. What must have been an old reception counter was, on one side, part of the kitchen, and on the other, a large stone fireplace.

Pointing to the counter, Andy said, "I'm sure you've guessed this must have been some kind of reception area. There used to be an office beyond it. As you can see, I've torn down the office wall and turned the area into a kitchen. I kept the old counter to act as a pass-through."

He paused then and looked around as if assessing it through her eyes. "Well, what do you think?"

Gina stepped into the room and walked around the large leather sofa and chairs that were arranged in front of the fire-place. It wasn't hard to imagine a group of fishermen telling tales in front of a roaring fire. She touched the worn leather on one of the chairs. "It's a great room. The furniture must be very old."

Andy was delighted she'd noticed the furniture. He pointed to a chair. "Sit down on that one."

Gina relaxed into the softness of the old leather. "Now," said Andy, "Lean back."

As Gina leaned, the chair gently tilted and a foot rest

came up. She couldn't help but gurgle with laughter as she found herself, somewhat swamped in the large chair, almost horizontal.

"They're really quite old and valuable," said Andy proudly. "All I had to do to restore them was work on the leather, which had gathered a lot of dust." Holding his hand out, he said, "Come on. I'll show you the rest of the house."

Under the staircase, on one side, was a door that led into a large room used for storage. It also contained a freezer, washer and dryer, and shelves of supplies. Beside it was a bathroom and beyond it, another small room that had obviously been used as an office.

Then they headed up the stairs. At the top, a short hall led into three rooms. The center room faced the front. This was obviously the master bedroom. The large dormer gave a clear view of the lake. On the pine plank floor, a very thick round rag rug gave the room warmth. Next to it was the bed and on the other side a dresser and highboy. Again, the furniture was old but glowed with evidence of loving care.

"The furniture was also in the lodge when I bought it. It needed a lot of work to restore it."

The mattress was bare and the fact that the room had no evidence of habitation made it seem lonely. Gina wondered if Andy had lived here with his wife. Had she died here on that very bed? Gina shivered with the thought. The idea spoiled her enjoyment of the lovely room.

Andy strolled over to the window. He said, almost to himself, "This house saved my sanity. When Kelly died, I couldn't bear to stay in the house we had in town. Carolyn found this place and suggested that I look at it. I knew the minute I saw it that it was for me."

Gina couldn't help the rush of relief she felt at this news.

Its effect frightened her. Why should it mean so much to her? What was she doing here? Andy seemed so intent on wanting her to like the house. She did like it, but why did that matter to him?

She suddenly felt she was way out of her depth. Why had she let him hold her hand? She liked the contact with him, but what did it mean? It wasn't as if they had ever dated. She had no idea how he felt about her. And how did she feel about him?

She looked over at him, still watching out the window. She knew she was attracted to him, but how did she *feel* about him? She'd learned that finding a man that was handsome and well-mannered wasn't enough. Dan had been all of that and a thoroughly fine person on top of it. But she knew now she hadn't loved him. She'd just been swept away with the idea of having someone like Dan pay attention to her.

So what was it she felt about Andy? She looked at him again, the noon sun shining in the window, lighting the chestnut tones in his hair, touching the lines of his forehead, cheek and chin. In spite of herself, she was drawn to him and without knowing how, she found herself standing by him, looking out the window. He turned to her and watched her gravely. Then he gave her one of his blue-eyed smiles, and she was lost. At that moment, she knew, without a doubt, that she cared for this man; this man who had suffered great loss and yet could find it in his heart to be concerned about her health and well-being. She recalled all the things he had done for her, all the understanding he had shown in the winter and now. But did she *love* him?

Suddenly shy, she turned away. "What's in the rest of the rooms?"

At her question, his face lit with enthusiasm. "Guess where the bathroom is?"

Gina looked around but couldn't see any door.

"Come with me," he said and marched toward the wall. Reaching out, he pulled a handle she hadn't noticed on the log wall and a door swung open to reveal an old-fashioned washroom with a tub on brass claws and an equally dated sink. "All the fixtures are old. I had to hunt all over the countryside to find them. I got quite interested in antiques as I searched."

Gina noticed another door on the other side. "What's on the other side of the door?"

Andy stepped forward and opened the door. Peeking through, she could see a smaller bedroom. "This will be a guest room. The only disadvantage is that the guests will have to share the washroom." Then he added as an afterthought, "It could also be a child's room."

Gina's imagination was immediately swamped with the picture of a dark-haired little boy with vivid blue eyes standing at the sink trying to reach the soap.

"You're smiling," observed Andy.

"I was just imagining a little kid trying to reach the soap or turn on the water."

"Oh," said Andy gravely, "I'd have to make a small stool for him or her to stand on."

They looked at each other and then Gina turned away. The thought of a small child, of a real family was too terrifyingly wonderful to entertain. Hastily, she stepped into the other room. "You haven't furnished it yet."

"I have to find some old pieces."

Andy led her to the room on the other side of the master

bedroom. It had a bed and dresser. It also had signs of people coming and going: a pair of swimming goggles and a towel over a chair. Andy explained, "Some of my family come out in the summer to swim. Let's get our lunch and see if it's warm enough to sit on the deck and get a tan."

Gina helped Andy bring out a table, umbrella, and chairs from a nearby shed. In the inside storage room, he found cushions for the chairs and a lounger. While Gina cleaned off the furniture, Andy brought the cooler from the car. He brought dishes from the kitchen, and they sat at the table, the umbrella tipped so they could enjoy the sunshine.

"You're a good cook," said Gina as she gobbled up sandwiches, celery, and pickles.

"I cannot tell a lie," said Andy. "Nora made them. I really don't know what I'm going to do when she goes off with my father."

Mentioning Nora made Gina remember that Merry had been looking at his father's house. "Do you know if Merry is going to buy the house?"

"She is. That's the first thing I meant to tell you." He grinned. "But then you mentioned wearing shorts and I lost my train of thought."

Gina enjoyed the compliment. Looking up at the sun, she said, "It's warm enough to wear them, but if we're going for a walk, I think I'll leave my jeans on." Instead, she pulled a chair over and placed her bare feet on it, wiggling her toes with enjoyment in the sunshine.

After they had eaten, Andy brought in the boxes from the car and together they unpacked. There were linens that she put in a large closet upstairs. There was also a box of his clothing he placed in the high boy in the bedroom. When they finished all the unpacking, they headed out for a walk.

Andy led Gina along a path that paralleled the shore. In places, the ice was out farther and ducks were busy diving. They came around a corner, and suddenly, Andy reached out and touched her arm, signaling for her to stop. Cautiously, he pointed. There, in a spot where the ice was still against the shore, a log was sticking up. Around the log a small pool of water had formed and, standing in it, motionless, was a great blue heron.

They stood, transfixed until the long-legged bird suddenly stepped forward and speared a fish. They watched as it expertly gulped down its lunch and then, with a squawk, pumped its wings and lifted off in ungainly flight over the ice until it reached a height where it could arrow its way out of sight.

Gina turned to Andy, her smokey eyes aglow with delight. "That was wonderful."

"And the show's not over. Listen."

Overhead in the pines, Gina suddenly became aware of a chorus of high, light notes above her head. "Watch," Andy instructed.

Gina watched and sure enough, she was able to pick out tiny grey birds moving from branch to branch. "What are they?" she whispered.

"Golden-crowned kinglets. See if you can spot their crowns."

"They're so tiny," she said, "oh, I see a crown," and then added, "thank you, Andy, for sharing all this with me."

Andy grabbed her hand again and said, "My pleasure. We'll have to come out again. This part of the forest is especially nice in a few weeks. The wild flowers are lovely here."

Together, they made their way back to the lodge. As they approached the deck, Andy again suddenly stood still. Gina stopped. He seemed to be listening to something. And then she heard it. It was as if a thousand chandeliers were tinkling in the wind.

"What is it?" she whispered.

"The ice. Look, it's starting to move. Let's get up on the deck. We'll see it better from there."

The ice was moving. Gina could see it slowly glide away from the shore. For a long time they watched as the ice, accompanied by a symphony of sounds, eased its way out of their sight.

Gina realized suddenly that Andy had come to stand beside her, his hand on her shoulder. It felt so right. It was all that she could do not to lean into him. Turning to her, he said, "I've never seen it go out like that before. Never heard the music."

Finally, they packed up and headed down the road back to town. Andy looked over at Gina only to discover that she'd fallen asleep. One hand lay opened on her lap, the other drooped over the side of the seat. Andy wondered what she thought of their trip. Had she enjoyed the day? She seemed to have. Would she want to spend part of her life out at the lake? Could she leave her new home for part of the time? He had already dreamed of them living in both places. Weekdays in the village and weekends and holidays at the lake. Images of small children enjoying the beach filled his head. Could he make his dream hers also?

Andy brought the van to a stop at the side of her house and looked over at Gina. The cessation of motion had no effect on her. She was still in a deep sleep. Not surprising, Andy thought, considering how sick she'd been mere days before.

He reached over and touched her cheek with the side of his hand. "Gina," he whispered. "We're home."

No response.

Getting out of the van, Andy went around it and opened the passenger side. "Gina," he said and touched her hand in her lap. The only response was a tiny noise, more a snuffle than a snore, then silence.

Bemused now, Andy thought, *she's going to have a fit if I carry her to bed again.* Deciding to do all the other tasks first, he left her, took her bag, and headed for the house. He still had his key, so he opened it and marched into the kitchen.

Inside, the house was quite chilly, so he started the fire and fed the kittens, who were anxious to play and interested in everything he did. Finally, when he could think of nothing else to do, he headed back out to the van.

Gina had not moved. "Gina," he said, quite loudly this time, "we're home." Again no response.

Fighting down the notion that he couldn't wait to feel her in his arms and going, instead, with the thought that he must get her inside, that she couldn't sleep there all evening, he gingerly reached over and lifted her.

Gina was not heavy. He already knew that. He shifted her so that her head rested against his shoulder, his other arm under her knees. For a moment, he waited for a reaction but got none. Her hair was just under his face and he was surrounded by her scent; a delicious mix of fresh air and wild flowers.

Duty calls, he thought to himself, ignoring the fact that he couldn't be more pleased to have a moment with Gina when she wasn't shying away like a startled doe. He managed the door and was sidling along the hallway when she sighed and opened her eyes.

For a second, he felt as if he'd been caught with his fingers in the cookie jar and waited for her reaction, but instead, she stared at him, her eyes luminous in the gloom of the hall, her sweet mouth slightly parted as she made sense of her situation.

Again, she sighed, and Andy was lost. Before he could stop himself, he bent his head and touched her lips with his. When she didn't push away, he leaned in closer. She was kissing him back, holding nothing back as she responded.

Trembling, he leaned back against the hall. Then he felt her tense up. Pushing herself away from his chest, she gave him an almost frightened look, as if she didn't know exactly what she was doing.

Easing her to her feet, Andy kept his hands on her shoulders. "I'm not going to apologize for kissing you," he said. "You were far too lovely to resist."

Again she looked at him out of those eloquent eyes and then with a shake of her head, hurried down the hall to the kitchen.

What, no response? he thought.

He followed her into the kitchen where she busied herself letting the kittens out of their cage. She was not going to look at him. He could see that.

"I fed the kittens and started the fire."

"Thank you," she mumbled, still keeping her back to him. "And thank you for the lovely day."

But not for the kiss, he thought. However, he also thought with some satisfaction, *she didn't slap my face.* Peeking around so that he could see a little of her face, he saw that she was blushing.

Taking pity on her, he started down the hall. "I promised I'd help my dad this evening. See you for a lesson tomorrow after work."

Gina listened to the van back out and start up the street. Refusing to think about what had just happened, she busied herself with putting away the things she had taken with her. Finally, there was nothing else to do. In a moment of panic, she decided to do a laundry. Hurrying into the bathroom, she lifted clothes from the hamper and was about to head across the hall to the washing machine when she caught her reflection in the mirror.

She was stunned. She looked different: aglow, radiant. In spite of herself, she touched her lips, lips that seemed fuller and redder. What had she been thinking when she let Andy kiss her like that? Even more perturbing, what had she been thinking when she kissed him back? And kiss him back she had, as if her life had depended on it.

She saw the fingers at her lips tremble and swiftly dropped her hand. Dan had given her the odd peck, but now she realized that they could have hardly been called kisses. More like tokens of friendship. But this kiss, the one Andy and she had shared, was something completely different. It was as if they had come together, meshed, welded, melded together.

In a daze, she headed back to her rocker and, picking up the kittens, ignored them as they played with her fingers, intent rather upon trying to figure out what it all meant.

It was 10:00 and Andy, Carolyn, David, Ben, Mike, and his wife, Naomi, had been working away around the house, following their father's direction. He'd decided what he wanted to take with him and given them his reasons, but his choices had scarcely scratched the surface of the house's contents; objects that had become symbols of their lives.

At that moment, they were all staring at the large buffet and china cabinet in the dining room. Mike, who was the oldest, had taken on the role of leader. Under his guidance, it had been decided that he and Naomi would like the dining room furniture; a relief to the rest of them who had no place to use it and yet didn't wish it to be sold.

Opening the doors of the buffet, Mike revealed an exquisite set of Limoges china. Carolyn couldn't help herself. She reached in and picked up a cup and saucer. A delicate mauve flower patterned the porcelain. Suddenly, she had tears in her eyes. "I can remember Mom having the ladies in and serving them lunch with this china. The set belonged to her mother's mother and she was very proud of it."

She held up the cup to the light and they could all see through its delicate shape. "I wish so much that I could ask to have this, but David's grandmother gave us a set of Royal Worcester china that belonged to her. It's quite lovely and suits us perfectly. Doesn't it, David?"

Obviously concerned because she was upset, he touched her shoulder. "You know, my grandmother wouldn't mind if you had two sets."

Carolyn shook her head. "I think someone else in the family should have it."

She looked at Ben. Maybe his fiancée, Barbara, would like it? He held up his hands in refusal. "Not me. Barbie has already picked out china she wants. Her taste is very modern, and I'm quite happy with that."

Carolyn looked at Mike and Naomi. They shook their heads. Together, the group turned and looked at Andy.

Trying hard to keep the blush he felt lurking, he said gruffly, "I'll take the set of dishes if no one else wants them. I think they're beautiful." He was talking quickly, because he didn't want his perceptive siblings guessing why he wanted the set. He just knew that it was perfect for Gina. He was sure she would love to have it in her house in town. Of course, that all depended on whether he could convince her to marry him. He knew that he couldn't give it to her without that guarantee. His brothers and sister would not be happy to see it leave the family.

Carolyn put down the cup and saucer and threw herself in his arms. "Oh, I'm so happy for you, Andy."

Inwardly rolling his eyes, Andy tried to rescue the situation, although he knew exactly what the others were thinking. "Because I'm taking Mom's china?"

Pulling herself together, Carolyn backed off. "Of course. It will look terrific among your antiques out at the lake."

But Andy knew that Carolyn had guessed his reason for wanting the china. It had nothing to do with his place at the lake. Was he that transparent? Did they all expect him to announce he was marrying Gina? *Well*, he thought glumly, *they might just be in for a surprise*. He had no idea if she'd agree to such a plan.

When they had chosen everything they wanted, they were still faced with the problem of how to dispose of the rest of the things in the house, especially things like duplicates in the kitchen and elsewhere. Finally, Naomi suggested, "Let's have a garage sale. If we had it as soon as possible, it would probably be one of the earliest in the season. We could hold it on the front lawn."

Carolyn was immediately enthusiastic. "That's a terrific

idea. We'll all have to help. Pray for a sunny day. If it's raining, we'll have to put it off a week, but that's getting pretty
close to the wedding and closing date."

Naomi was an organizer and soon had them all responsible
for some part of the sale, but as Andy made his way upstairs to
the third floor, he wondered just how they could possibly have
the house ready for Merry in time. And then the picture of
Gina pouring tea into the delicate cups flashed across his
imagination and he smiled. The china was made for her. Now
he just had to convince her that she was made for him.

Andy considered his strategies. When he thought of it, he
was surprised to realize that it had only been two weeks
since that morning when he'd walked into the clinic and
teased her. However, he'd met Gina first at Carolyn and
David's housewarming the Christmas before. Over the winter, he'd watched her as she frantically tried to hold on to
Dan and had supported her when her efforts had collapsed.
Obviously, some recognition that Gina was important to him
had been operating long before now.

Considering the time factor, it was no wonder Gina was
wary around him. And, of course, that kiss hadn't helped.
On the other hand, he thought with a grin, he wasn't the least
bit sorry. After that kiss, there should be no doubt in her
mind that he was interested in her.

So what should he do next? Ask her for a date? That
hardly seemed right. After all, he would be around getting
his computer lessons and working on the wiring. It seemed
almost overkill to consider dating. Yet how else did a man let
a woman know he was interested?

Kelly and he had been friends all through high school. In
time, that friendship had developed into love. Andy realized

that he'd probably never had to work at starting up a relationship. The thought of asking for a date actually made him nervous.

He had a feeling that Gina had to get used to him. Instead of dating, he decided on another strategy. Because of the wiring and computer lessons, he would be *in her face* and yet at the same time, he would *keep his distance*. He needed to observe her, to see if that attraction that bubbled between them would develop more substance. But he would keep it light and easy for now.

When Gina walked into the clinic the next morning with the kittens in their cage, she was met with cheers from all the staff present.

Ted rushed forward to take the kittens from her while Merry called her to hurry over to the counter. When Gina got behind it, she found out why. "Look," said Merry. "A plant came for you not ten minutes ago. I wonder who sent it?"

Excitement surged through Gina. Surely it was from Andy. And then she began to doubt herself. She felt herself blushing as she opened the plant. It was a beautiful fuchsia-colored cyclamen.

Ted pointed, "Look, Gina. There's a card tucked in the paper around the pot."

They all waited as she picked it up and opened it. She read it and felt her face glow with embarrassment.

"Well," they said in unison. "Who sent it?"

Tucking the card away in her pocket, she said as coolly as she could. "Andy." Then improvising, she added, "He said, 'Glad you're back to work. Can't wait until our next lesson.'"

But that was not the truth. What it had said was "Glad

you're back to work. From Andy, who is not the least bit sorry he kissed you yesterday."

Gina heard a drill and then the sound of men's voices. She heard Andy laugh and it made her jumpy. For ten days now, he seemed to be around all the time, either at the house or the clinic. Every moment he was around, she was unbearably aware of him. She loved the sound of his laughter and the way he would tease her when she was helping him with his computer skills. Yet, at no time did he act like he had before, as if she was special to him. He made no attempt to hold her hand or kiss her, just the occasional casual touch if she was in his way or if he wanted her attention. And he certainly had not asked her out for supper or taken her to a movie. When she'd thanked him for the flowers he sent to the clinic, he just grinned.

And yet, she was sure something was percolating between them. At night, she dreamed of him. In the daytime, thoughts of him intruded into her work, making her make silly mistakes.

Finally she started leaving him in the house working on the bright spring evenings and going over to help Cindy with the tearoom. It was to open on the very day that Jim Thompson married Nora. Because of the rush to get the Thompson house ready, Carolyn and the rest of the family were helping there rather than at the tearoom.

Cindy's tearoom was really taking shape. Walls had been painted, the hardwood floors refinished and windows cleaned. Furniture and linens had been purchased. Gina had made a poster from pictures Dan and Cindy had taken of the tearoom and these were appearing around town. Gina had sent information to the local papers advertising the tearoom.

An elegant sign had been made and placed on the lawn in front of the tearoom.

Gina enjoyed helping but, at the same time, wanted to be at home when Andy was there. However, when he was there, she felt the urge to flee to the tearoom.

Tonight was no different. She felt just as edgy. Glancing at her watch, she saw that it was time for her to make the two men coffee. When it was ready, she climbed the creaky stairs that led to the second floor. Here she found that Nick had climbed up through the access door and into the attic. Andy was standing on the ladder and calling out instructions. Then she heard a scraping in the wall. Seconds later, there was a cheer from the attic. "I've got the wire," she heard Nick say in triumph.

Suddenly, Andy seemed to realize she was watching. He turned and said, "Successful fishing, Gina. Now, we're really going to make some headway."

"Do you think you could stop for some coffee and cookies?" Gina asked.

"Chocolate chip?" asked Andy.

"What else? I know you Thompsons are all addicted to them."

Gina was amused at the speed with which the two men stopped their work and headed for the kitchen.

As Nick walked through the door, Midnight pounced on his foot. Startled, Nick looked down and laughing, picked up his feline assailant. Midnight wiggled and managed to crawl up on to his shoulder where he hung down while watching for the other kittens. He was not disappointed. The orange and the tabby came charging across the room. Without warning, Midnight took a flying leap off Nick, lighting on a chair and then projecting himself after his brother and sister.

"Boy, are they ever getting rowdy," observed Andy.

Gina watched the kittens fondly as they scrambled about after each other. "They're always lively about now. In a few moments, they'll fall asleep."

Once everyone had a coffee and was munching on a cookie, Gina asked, "Nick, how is school coming? I haven't seen you around the library lately."

Nick gave her a radiant look. "I'm finished. Passed my course."

Andy added, "Got an A plus. Nick, you must be good to get a grading that high."

Nick blushed and took another cookie.

Still interested, Gina said, "What do you plan to do now?"

If Nick had been radiant before, now he positively glowed with happiness. "I'm going to start my apprenticeship to be an electrician. Andy has been letting me work evenings to gain experience. His apprentice, Tim, has just completed all his work and passed his exams and is now a qualified electrician. Andy has offered to sponsor me."

Gina glanced at Andy who had just headed for the coffee pot. *He's embarrassed*, she thought, and cared for him all the more because of it. Looking at Nick, she said, "Congratulations. Just for that I'll make you up a box of cookies to take home."

As Gina was making up the box, Andy said, "I wondered if you'd be free to help with the garage sale."

Gina's heart lifted. Everyone had been talking about it, but no one had suggested she help. Even Merry, Ruth, and the two little boys planned to be there. After all, Merry had explained, she really couldn't do much in the way of preparation until she got the house and could move her belongings in.

"Sure. What time?"

"You probably should be there about seven-thirty. We've advertised 'not before eight' but I'm sure there will be people there a lot earlier."

"What if it rains?" asked Nick.

"We've been watching the weather report and the weekend looks like it will be ideal," said Andy.

"I wouldn't mind helping," said Nick. "If you're setting out tables and things, I'll be free on Friday night to help and Saturday too."

"Thanks, Nick. I'm sure we can use the help."

"Oh, and by the way," Andy added, "We're serving coffee and muffins Saturday morning for all our helpers. Cindy has offered to send them over, although I don't know how she'll find time to make them."

Andy watched Gina carefully as she snagged a kitten that was trying to climb up the pedestal of the table they sat around. He couldn't resist saying, "Gina, why don't you bring the cage over with the kittens. It would be an ideal time to find them a home."

She looked stricken and clutched the kitten to her heart. "But I couldn't . . . that is I'm not going . . . I'm going to keep them," she said defiantly, daring anyone to contradict her.

Andy grinned. "Somehow, I was sure you would."

She glowered some more at him and put the kitten in the cage, then hurried after the other ones and placed them back in the cage also. "I'm used to them," she muttered. "I care for them."

Then she glanced over at him, her chin up, ready for an argument, only to realize that he was laughing at her. "You're teasing," she accused.

He laughed. "Yes, little mother."

With that, he stood and said, "Guess that's all we can do tonight, Nick. We might as well pack up."

Andy whistled away to himself as he disappeared down the hall with Nick close behind. He just loved teasing her.

Chapter Nine

Andy had been right. The weather was perfect, Gina decided, as she parked her bicycle safely away in a shed at the back of the Thompson property. There wasn't even a hint of a cloud in the sky. Trees and shrubs were even more vivid in their spring colors as buds began to swell, ready to burst the first time the temperature stayed warm for several days.

There were already people poking about at the tables, so she hurried out to the front of the house where Carolyn greeted her. "Do you think you could manage the cash?" she asked.

Gina nodded. "No problem."

"Help yourself to some food and then I'll show you how we have it organized."

Once she had her coffee and muffin, Gina made her way to the table that was obviously intended for the cashier. "If you're not sure about something, ask Naomi. The price is written on a white tag glued to each object." Carolyn pointed out her sister-in-law.

Gina nodded. She knew Naomi from the clinic. The family had a black lab.

For the next two hours, Gina barely had time to look up. Everyone in town seemed to be at the sale. Strangers, having read of the sale in the newspaper, were also taking advantage of the bargains. Gina had only taken time off to buy a toaster, much newer than the one she had, and an electric beater.

Now, the action was slowing down a bit and she began to watch the shoppers. Laughter made her look over at a table that still held a pile of odds and ends. A petite blonde yelled, "Give it to me, Andy," and than began chasing him around the yard until she had him cornered against the hedge that edged the verandah. Gina watched as the woman threw herself at him and tried to snatch at a battered old teddy bear he held up high.

"No way," said Andy. "You can't have it. Not unless you pay a forfeit."

The woman stood before him, her hands on her hips, laughing. "So what's the forfeit?"

"Well, a kiss, of course."

Gina's heart turned a somersault and then clenched in dismay as the pretty woman leaned forward and took his head between her hands, stood on tiptoe, and kissed him—right on the mouth. Scowling, Gina looked away. So, he had time to flirt with other women. Pretty women.

Andy, watching her, felt a great surge of triumph. She was jealous. He was sure she was. Grabbing Barbie's hand, for it was Ben's fiancée that he had been chasing, he took her over to Gina.

"Gina," he said, "Do you remember Barbie?"

Gina pasted a phony smile on her face and said, "Barbie? I don't think so."

"Barbie is Ben's fiancée. She's been studying in Toronto. She only just made it up here."

Then Gina remembered that she had actually met Barbie at Carolyn and David's housewarming back in the winter. This time she gave her a genuine smile.

Holding up a bedraggled teddy bear, Andy said, "I think Barbie wants to buy this old teddy that belonged to Ben." With a bow, he handed the bear to Barbie.

Gina was sure her relief must be evident as she made change for Barbie. She'd never felt jealousy like this before. Not even when Dan made it clear he loved Cindy. For a few moments there, she had wanted to tear Barbie's eyes out.

Subdued by thoughts of her jealousy, Gina tried to distract herself by adding up the cash that had come in so far.

More laughter intruded on her calculations, and when she glanced up, she saw Merry and Ruth, her nanny, with their children Michael and Jimmy. The two boys were busy looking at boxes of games that still remained while Ruth and Merry checked out items that interested them: pieces of glassware, lamps and books. Gina watched as Ruth returned to the tables with the lamps and chose a table lamp. Holding it up, she called to Merry, "I think I could use this in the apartment." She checked it out and then said, "Oh, dear. It really needs rewiring."

Nick appeared in a flash by Ruth's side. Turning to him, Ruth said, "Oh, hi, Nick. I don't think I've seen you since high school. Are you still living over in Buchanan?"

"No, I moved to Stewart's Falls after my mother remarried." Pointing to the lamp, he asked, "What's wrong with the wiring?"

Ruth held up the wire. "It's dried out and brittle. I'm afraid it will cause a fire."

Ruth looked at him with surprise when he said, "Let me check the lamp. I'm pretty handy. I'll fix it for you."

Observing this exchange, Gina thought, *Nick has good taste.* Ruth was a very pretty woman. Very feminine with light brown hair that hung down to her shoulders and large hazel eyes. When she hesitated, Nick said, "Check with Andy. He'll tell you I know how. Here, give me the lamp."

Obviously bemused, Ruth handed him the lamp and watched while he checked it over. Handing it back to her, he said, "If you'll trust me with it, I'll have it fixed for you in no time. No charge."

Gina saw that Ruth was blushing as she gave him the lamp. Maybe something would come of this meeting, she thought.

Finally, about 2:00, they closed the sale. In no time, the tables disappeared and objects that had not sold were stored away. Jim and Nora had arranged for a feast in the backyard so as tasks were finished, people hurried there.

Gina had just finished adding up the amount raised when Andy came over and took her hand. "Come on. I've reserved the best seat in the house for us."

Surprised by this reversion to his former behavior, she let herself be led to the backyard. Here, the sun poured through lacy branches of maples and oaks not quite ready to bud, warming everyone. Protected by the house and out of the breeze that had kept everything cool throughout the morning, people were taking off heavy sweatshirts.

Andy led her to a wooden swing just big enough for two. It was set on a platform and glided magically back and forth. Andy put his shirt over the back to mark ownership and then they headed toward the food.

Nora had arranged the food on a round table on the deck.

Nearby, Andy's father was busy barbecuing hamburgers and hot dogs. "I'm glad the weather has been so good. Dad's been dying to have the first barbecue of the year."

Together they lined up with the rest of the family and their friends for their hamburgers, then filled the rest of their plates with potato and bean salad.

Together, they sat on the swing, moving gently back and forth as they ate and chatted. Gina could not remember when she had been happier. For a little while, she was part of this family, enjoying their jokes and camaraderie. Andy, watching her, took pleasure in her obvious happiness.

Overhead, there was a sudden burst of song from a tree that spread its branches over the swing. Andy turned his head and listened. "A warbling vireo."

Gina squinted up through the branches on which buds were swelling. "Do you know all the birds? I can't see anything."

Andy leaned toward her, running one arm along the swing behind her and said, "Look at that large branch that leans toward the deck. Watch it carefully."

Gina caught sight of movement, of a tiny body moving along the top of the branch. The song filled the air again. "That bird, or maybe its offspring, has been coming here for years. It sings all spring and part of the summer."

Gina couldn't help it. She turned toward him only to find herself looking into his blue, blue eyes. She could drown in them, she thought. She was so dazzled that she missed his question.

"What did you say?" she asked.

"Will you come with me to my Father's wedding?"

Gina's heart leaped. Did he actually ask her to go with him to his Dad's wedding? To be part of his family's most important event?

"Well?" he asked.

Unable to stop the surge of delight that spread through her, she said, "I'd love to."

"Great!" said Andy. "I'll let you know all the details."

Then he glanced over to where the food was set out. A cooler had been added. As he watched, David came along with an ice cream scoop and lifted the lid. "Anyone for ice cream?"

Turning to Gina, he said, "Want an ice cream cone?"

Gina nodded and watched as Andy made his way over to David. She was so happy. She was going to the wedding with Andy. She watched as he laughed with David as the cones were made. A wisp of hair had escaped the tie he used to keep it back off his face. She was overcome with a sudden urge to go over and tuck it back behind his ear. Her fingers itched. What would his skin feel like? His ear? His hair?

He returned then and she was embarrassed. What if he could read her mind? Then she scolded herself for being silly and settled down on the swing with him to enjoy the rest of a wonderful day.

Just then, Michael and Jimmy ran up to Andy. "Did you finish your song?" Michael asked.

"You mean the song about the yellow cat?"

Both boys nodded their heads. Michael began to sing "A yellow bird sat on an orange cat's head" and Jimmy joined in.

Andy was surprised. "You both remember the words?"

"We do," they shouted with exuberance and began to sing,

> *"A yellow bird sat on an orange cat's head.*
> *" 'I wonder what's above,' the orange cat said.*
> *"Something good to eat?*
> *"Something good to crunch?*
> *"Will it make a good lunch?"*

By this time, Merry and Ruth had come up. "They've been singing that song ever since you taught it to them," said Merry. "Did you finish it?"

"Pretty well," said Andy. "There's the odd line missing, however, I think it doesn't matter. I'll go in and get my guitar and sing it for you."

Minutes later, Andy arrived back with his guitar. Pulling up a stool, he settled on it and took his instrument out of the case. For a moment or so, he tuned it, then winked at Gina and turned to the boys. "Okay, here goes. I'll sing it once and then you. I'll do it again so you can learn the other verses."

> *"A yellow bird sat on an orange cat's head,*
> *" 'I wonder what's above,' the orange cat said.*
> *" 'Something good to eat?*
> *" 'Something good to crunch?*
> *" 'What do you think ?*
> *" 'Will it make a good lunch?' "*

> *" 'Oh, dear, Oh dear,' the yellow bird said.*
> *" 'I didn't mean to land right on your head,*
> *" 'I'm not good to eat.*
> *" 'I'm not good to crunch.*
> *" 'You'll get sick if you eat me for lunch.' "*

The boys nodded their heads wisely at this. "Feathers don't taste good," Michael stated.

> *" 'Fly away yellow bird,' the orange cat said.*
> *" 'Fly away before I snatch you off my head.*
> *" 'Before I eat you up for lunch.*
> *" 'Before I have a real good crunch.' "*

" '*I think I will,' the yellow bird said.*
" '*Before I'm lunch.*
" '*Before you get a chance to crunch.*
" '*Goodbye orange cat. Goodbye all.*
" *I'm off to a tree that's very tall.' "*

Gina was fascinated by Andy's performance and the boys' responses. While he sang the new parts, the boys clapped to the beat. They laughed when Andy changed his voice for each character.

"He'll make a great father," a voice said at her shoulder. Looking around, Gina found Carolyn smiling as she watched the scene.

Gina could only nod with agreement. He certainly would. Images of two small boys sitting on Andy's lap came to mind.

"Would you like children?" Carolyn asked Gina.

Without thinking, Gina said, "Oh, yes. I want several." And then she blushed. Why had Carolyn asked her that?

As the afternoon cooled, people moved inside. Soon, the family was talking about the wedding. Jim and Nora had been lucky to find a place for the reception. As Jim explained, "Most places around here that accommodate are fully booked by now. It was Cindy who suggested we call The Pines. Surprisingly enough, they had space for a reception. They explained that, although the Victorian Day holiday is usually busy, this year they've got an opening, and that they'd be willing to have our reception there."

Gina listened while they discussed the details of the wedding. Slowly, it sank in that this was going to be a small but very classy affair. Caroline and Naomi were busy discussing what they planned to wear. It soon became apparent that they were planning a major shopping event. Suddenly, all Gina's happiness at being invited to the wedding began to fade. How was she going to afford a new dress? And new shoes? She didn't even have a good spring coat. Just a light jacket that she wore everywhere.

Andy noticed that the happiness she had expressed when he asked her to go had faded and that she was sitting there, nibbling her lower lip and looking miserable. What had put her off?

Shortly after, people began to head for home. Gina turned to him and said, "It's time I went home. The kittens have been alone all day. I'm sure they'll have gobbled up all the food I left."

"Fine," said Andy. "I'll take you."

"But I have my bike. It's just out in the shed at the back."

"No problem," said Andy. "I'll just tuck it into the van." *And*, he thought, *I'll try to find out just what is worrying you.*

When they reached her house, Gina hopped out and hurried to the door. Andy reached into the van, lifted out the bike, and put it in her storage shed. Then, he followed her into the house. It was cold.

Not for long, he decided. He was going to get at least one line in so that he could install a wall heater in the kitchen.

Gina was busy putting down food for the kittens, so Andy headed to the stove. It was completely out, so he busied himself getting a fire started. When he'd succeeded, he turned to where Gina rocked away in her chair, a kitten in her lap.

"What's troubling you, Gina?"

She stood at that and put the kitten back in the cage,

something it objected to loudly, especially since its siblings were tearing around the room.

Not to be put off, Andy came over to where she stood looking out over the darkened garden. "What is it?"

Still staring out the window, she said, "Nothing."

Andy placed a hand on her shoulder and turned her towards him. "Are you having second thoughts about the wedding?"

"I . . . No. I'm looking forward to it." But how could she go with him? She didn't want to embarrass him. She didn't have anything suitable to wear to a wedding. She looked at him, trying to find the words to tell him she couldn't go, but they simply wouldn't leave her lips.

Andy looked into her troubled eyes and sighed. He saw right through her. She wasn't going to share her problem. Changing tactics, he lifted her chin and kissed her; it was a long, gentle kiss of caring and assurance. Then, he held her to him, wrapped his arms around her and said, "Someday, you'll trust me. Whatever the problem is, I'm sure a solution can be found."

Stepping away from her, he headed toward the hall. "I want to help my Dad tomorrow morning, but if it's alright with you, I'll come over in the afternoon to work on the wiring." Before she could object, he disappeared out the door.

Suddenly, Gina was exhausted. Taking pity on the lone kitten in the cage, she let it out and sat back down in her rocker. Unable to fight her despair, she let the tears fall. She'd wanted so much to lean on Andy and let him solve all her problems. It had been such a temptation. But how could she say, *I can't afford a dress? In fact, I can't afford the wiring*. The hope that the requested grant would materialize seemed to have as much chance of happening as she had of getting a new dress.

When Andy arrived back home, he found his Dad busy sorting out the money from the garage sale into four piles.

"What on earth are you doing?" Andy asked.

"Four kids, four piles."

"Four kids?" asked Andy trying to count up grandchildren and not getting four.

"Mike, Carolyn, Ben, and you. I certainly don't need the money." As he spoke, he split one of the piles in half. "You may each do whatever you like with your share. If you have any sense, you'll split your share with Gina. She worked as hard as any of us. I gather you asked her to the wedding. She might need the money to get something to wear."

Andy couldn't believe he'd been so stupid. *Of course, that was what was worrying Gina!* "How did you guess that was what upset her?"

"Nora was listening to Naomi and Carolyn talk about what they intended to wear to the wedding. Seemed they were planning one great old shopping trip. Nora said she couldn't help but notice Gina's expression."

"You tell Gina I want her to have the money," Jim said. "I think she feels too beholden to you already."

Monday morning, Gina found herself run off her feet with emergencies. It didn't seem possible that so many pets could get into so much trouble in one weekend. By noon, when the last of the creatures with their owners had left, she was exhausted. As she checked to see if her records were correct after the morning's whirlwind of activity, Dan walked in from the back.

"That was one wild morning. How are you holding up?"

Gina waved the record book. "I think I've got everything accounted for. Run your eye down it and see if I've missed anything."

Dan came over and glanced down the pages. "Looks good to me." Then, turning to Gina, he teased, "Hear you were at the garage sale and worked like a demon. Also heard you sat with Andy on the swing."

Gina blushed.

Dan studied his diminutive receptionist. It was silly, but he felt responsible for her. He remembered her unhappiness in the winter and admired the brave way she had met her troubles head on. He knew that her presence in the clinic made it run like clockwork. Her happiness mattered. He couldn't help prying a little.

"How do you feel about Andy, Gina?"

Gina supposed he had the right to ask such a personal question. She'd certainly intruded in his love life only a few months before. Looking at Dan with worried eyes, she said, "I like him very much. But as you know, I'm not too smart at understanding exactly how I feel."

"Do you love him?"

Suddenly, the answer was simple. "I do," she heard herself say and knew she was blushing even harder than before. 'But," she added, "I don't know how he feels."

At that, Dan laughed. "You're kidding."

"It's not funny, Dan. As you know, I'm not too smart about these things. Just look how I misunderstood you."

Dan became serious at that. "Gina. Use your head. Think about all the things Andy has done for you in the past month.

He's made sure you could get back and forth from work with the kittens. He stayed with you when you were sick. I understand that he's working on your wiring, and he helped you make out a grant application. What does he have to do to make you see that he cares?"

"Well," she mumbled. "I need to be told. A woman likes to know."

"And so does a man," countered Dan. With that, he turned and made his way toward the back. "Leave that stuff and come on and eat."

Ignoring the order, Gina flopped in her chair. Had she just said she loved Andrew Thompson? She had, and it was true. In one way, it was a relief to admit it to herself. She realized that she'd loved him when he'd teased her with his April Fools' joke. But she'd loved him even before that. Thinking back to when he came to her during the winter and helped her face her despair, she must have fallen in love with him then. The problem was that she'd felt so bad about her actions toward Dan and Cindy that she'd often avoided Andy, along with everyone else in town. It had only been since the transportation of the kittens and the wiring of the house that she had been able to relax with him and let her feelings grow.

But how did he feel? Everything Dan said about Andy was true. But then, he was a genuinely nice person and might well have done the same for anyone. And how did she show Andy that she cared for him? How could she take the risk?

By the end of a remarkably quiet afternoon at the clinic, Gina had caught up with her work and was anxiously waiting for Andy. He'd worked furiously all the previous afternoon and announced with triumph just before he left that he was ready to connect a heater in her kitchen. He just had to pick up one, he'd said, and she'd have heat when it became too warm to use the stove.

Again she worried about money. It was too early to expect the grant to come through. Now he was buying a wall heater. And what about the dress for the wedding?

At that point in her worries, Andy came hurrying in. "Move over, Teach. I've got a lot to practice before tomorrow."

Gina got out of his way and watched how he settled at the computer and turned it on. He confidently worked through the steps that took him into the program he wanted to use. Grinning at Gina, he said, "See, Teach. I've done my homework."

"So you have," she replied. But when she would have proceeded to show him something new, he took an envelope out of his shirt pocket and said, "Oh, before I forget, my Dad asked me to give this to you."

Mystified, Gina took the envelope. Reaching for a letter opener, she sliced the top and pulled out a letter folded in three with something in it. She opened the letter carefully and discovered that inside it there was money.

Confused, she looked at Andy. "What's this?"

"Read the letter."

Straightening out the paper, Gina read,

Gina, I've divided up the money we earned at the garage sale among Mike, Carolyn, Ben, Andy and you. I want you to have a share of this as you worked as hard as anyone else in the family. Thank you again for giving your time and energy. Jim Thompson.

Gina felt her face flame as she read the letter. Looking at Andy, she said, "I can't take this. It should go to the four of you."

Andy said, "Would you want to hurt my Dad's feelings?"

"No, of course not."

"Well, then, accept the money in the spirit it was given. He was very pleased that he could share the money with all of us. Now, let's get on with the lesson."

Even as they worked, Gina was imagining the dress she would wear to the wedding. Surely, if she was careful, she could get what she needed, and maybe even a wedding present.

Chapter Ten

Andy smiled as he heard Gina racing down the stairs from the second floor to get a tool for him. Three nights this week, he'd worked in the house and Gina had been with him all the way. She'd handed him tools, sat beside holes he'd made in her walls watching for the end of a wire, and supplied coffee and cookies in great quantities. She'd even taken part; screwing on face plates when a connection was finished and learning how to install a plug under his supervision.

He had never seen her happier. She chattered and teased. Occasionally, she would touch him. Once, when his ponytail came undone, she tied back his hair. Her fingertips on his nape as she gathered his hair together had driven him crazy. Another time, she insisted on looking after his hand when he'd scratched it on a piece of the old lath they had had to break through. She had been adorable, anxiously nibbling at her lip as she'd cleansed the cut. He'd desperately wanted to kiss those lips.

He loved this new, enthusiastic Gina. Her confidence delighted him. He was sure, now, that she loved him. She hadn't said so, but she acted like she cared for him.

He smiled again when he thought of the next day, Saturday. He had to go to a large building supply company in Smithboro to get material for a new job he was starting the following Monday. He'd casually mentioned he was going and asked if Gina would like to go too. Her face had lit up at the suggestion. She'd love to, she'd admitted. She wanted to look for some new clothes. Of course, she hadn't said she was shopping for the wedding, but he knew that was what she was thinking.

She hurried back up the stairs and, out of breath, handed him the tool. Laughing at her, he said, "Slow down, Gina. You'll exhaust yourself."

Kneeling down beside him, her eyes glowing, she said, "But I'm enjoying myself. I like working with you. I like learning how to do things. It's great."

Unable to resist her, he leaned over and gave her a quick kiss on her cheek. "I'm glad." Using the tool she'd brought up, he fished the final wire out for the last plug required in the room. "There, all I have to do is install the box and plug and the second floor is finished. You'll be able to use this room whenever you want now."

Gina sat back against the wall and looked about the room with its window looking over the neighbor's yard and its faded wallpaper. "Mmmm," she said, "I'm trying to imagine how I'll decorate this room. I wonder what I'll use it for?"

Andy thought to himself, *I have some suggestions but now is not the time to mention children.* He could see the room making a very nice nursery. Instead, he asked, "In what order do you see yourself refinishing these rooms?"

"Well, I think the rooms downstairs have to come first. I'd

like to use the one room at the front for a bedroom, the other for a living room. What do you think?"

Andy nodded. "I think that's a good plan. Then you could use the addition you sleep in now as a dining room or a study. There are lots of possibilities."

He finished installing a box and plug, then packed up this tools. "There, done for another evening. Time I was going."

She helped him pick up materials and led the way down the stairs. "What time do you want to leave in the morning?"

"Nine, if that's okay with you."

"I'll be ready."

Storing his materials in the laundry room, Andy turned to her and said softly, "It's been a great evening. We got a lot done." Then, taking her face in his hands, he said, "See you tomorrow, love," and kissed her goodnight.

When he'd disappeared out the door, Gina stood there, her fingers on her lips. "Love," he'd called her and her spirits rocketed. Twirling down the hall, she hurried into the kitchen. While letting the kittens out of their cage, she said, "He called me 'love.' What do you think? Do you think he knows? Have I made it plain enough?" Then, taking another whirl around the kitchen, she sang, *"I'm in love, I'm in love, I'm in love, I'm in love, I'm in love with a wonderful guy."* Nellie, the heroine from *South Pacific*, could not have been more in love than she was.

Andy peered through the window of his van, trying vainly to see his way as the windshield wipers did their best to clear the streamers of water caused by the heaviest rain showers he'd probably ever experienced. Beside him, Gina seemed utterly unconcerned about being soaked to the skin when she stepped out of the vehicle. A flash of lightning brightened the sky, followed by a clap of thunder that should have had her leaping in the air, but she remained still, humming a tune and dreamily watching the rain.

"Aren't you afraid you'll be drenched?" he asked.

Gina turned to him, obviously surprised by his remark. "No. I have a plastic rain coat. Anyway, I listened to the weather report this morning, and they said this storm would clear away and the next few days would be sunny and warm."

She started to hum again, and he couldn't resist asking, "What is that song? I know the tune but I can't quite place it."

She stopped humming abruptly and then mumbled, "I don't know. It's just something that was going through my head."

Andy glanced at her and was amused to see that she was looking embarrassed. What was that about?

Now they were heading into the center of the city of Smithboro. Large maple, oak and chestnut trees lined the older part of town, gracing the lawns of brick houses with wide front verandahs. Swollen buds weighed down the branches while, on some trees, leaves were actually beginning to open. The roads and sidewalks were covered with tiny clusters of maple blossoms that the rain had washed free. Early tulips and daffodils splashed vivid colors under the trees.

Moments later, they came to a stop in an area of stores that Gina had wanted to visit. Andy grinned. They were in front of a series of dress shops. "Are you sure you wouldn't like to shop out at the mall?" he asked, knowing full well that it was the dress shops she was interested in.

Gina was busy picking up her purse and a small plastic bag she'd brought with her. "No. This is exactly where I want to be. I'll phone you from a store when I've finished and let you know where I am. See you later." And with that, she was gone, springing across the sidewalk and under a store awning. She turned around, waved, and waited until he drove away before entering one of the stores.

As he made his way up the street, Andy found himself whistling the tune she'd been humming and suddenly he knew the words. She was singing one of the tunes from *South Pacific.* *"I'm in love, I'm in love, I'm in love with a wonderful guy."* His heart swelling with happiness, Andy headed off to get his supplies.

Gina waited until Andy disappeared, then stood in front of a store window, studying its contents. When she had said she was going to buy a dress for the wedding, Cindy had told her of this store. It was called Emily's Place, and everything was there on consignment. Looking at the display in the window, it was hard to believe. The dresses on the mannequins looked as if they cost a fortune.

A young woman was busy helping a customer near the back of the store, so Gina took a moment to survey the place, noting that the kind of dresses she was interested in were along one wall. She headed straight to the left end of the rack where a flash of periwinkle blue caught her eye. The tab at the top was her size. Holding her breath, she reached up and lifted the dress off the rack. It was everything she'd ever dreamed of.

The dress was as light as a feather. Touching the fabric, she was sure it was silk. Checking the tab, she saw that she was correct. Just then, a voice said, "Would you like to try the dress on?"

Startled, Gina found herself looking into the smiling face

of a young woman not much older than herself. "Oh, yes," Gina said. "It's exactly what I'm looking for. I hope it fits."

A few minutes later, Gina was standing in a cubicle, stripped down to her underwear and pantihose. Her fingers trembled as she took the dress off the hangar and slipped it over her head. The delicious fabric slid down her body and clung to her every curve as if it were made for her alone. She peeked at her back in the mirror and was surprised to discover that there was no zipper. Twisting about, she couldn't find it. At that moment, the salesgirl said, "Do you need any help?"

Opening the door, Gina said, "I can't find the zipper."

"Come out here and let me help. It's under your arm."

Seconds later, Gina found herself in front of a full-length mirror. The silk seemed to float around her. The dress had short, capped sleeves that were trimmed with a few frills that fluttered beguilingly as she turned around in front of mirror. The fitted waist flared out over the hip to move as she twisted this way and that. She felt the essence of spring.

The salesgirl sighed. "That is truly the most beautiful dress I've ever had in the store. It's as if it was made for you and no one else."

Gina didn't doubt her for a moment. It was as if the color emphasized everything good about her. Her hair seemed to shine more brightly, her eyes gleamed darkly, her cheeks were delicately tinted with pink.

Dreading to ask the question, Gina turned to the girl. She'd been so anxious to try it on that she'd forgotten to check the price. "How much is the dress?"

"Well, it is an original and it's never been worn, so I'm afraid it will cost a little more than most of the gowns."

Gina's heart sank. An original?

"The dress is a hundred and twenty-five dollars."

Gina stared at the dress and back at the saleslady. "You mean that?"

"Yes. I'm sorry it's so much, but the owner wants a good return and, of course, I have to cover my costs."

Gina could hardly keep back the tears of relief. "Sold," she said. "It's the most beautiful dress I've ever had on."

When Gina came out of the cubicle, the woman had the dress wrapped in tissue and was about to place it in a stylish box. She stopped what she was doing and said, "What kind of an affair are you wearing this dress to."

"A wedding."

"Well, let me show you what else we have that might suit you." Heading over to another rack, she said, "Do you have a spring coat?"

"No," said Gina, not sure she could afford anything else.

"I have just the coat for you. It's really a raincoat but it looks very classy. Very few people are your size and it's been hanging on the rack for some time." Taking an oyster-colored coat off the hanger, she held it out for Gina to try.

Putting down her purse and plastic bag, Gina slipped her arms into the coat and it settled on her shoulders like an extra skin. "Thirty dollars," said the woman.

"Only thirty dollars?" asked Gina.

"Marked down from fifty dollars."

"I'll take it."

By the time Gina had finished, she had a dress, coat, and scarf that were all made for each other. In another box, she had a pair of shoes matching the color of the dress. "The woman who brought in the dress and shoes is just your size. She is also very hard to please and did not like the dress. She only wears her things once but, this time, she didn't even try on the dress. I'm not sure what put her off. Possibly the color wasn't right," the sales girl explained.

Once Gina had paid for her purchases, she glanced at her watch. She had only been forty minutes. She was sure Andy knew why she had come to Smithboro and had resigned himself to several hours of cooling his heels.

"May I use your phone?" she asked with a smile of satisfaction.

Andy parked exactly where he'd let Gina off only fifty minutes earlier. He watched as she literally danced across the sidewalk and climbed into the van after first putting several brightly colored bags into the space behind her seat.

"Where to?" he asked, prepared to spend the entire day waiting while she shopped.

"I'm finished," she declared.

Andy did a double take. "You're finished?"

"Absolutely," she said smugly. "What do you think of that?"

Andy could only shake his head in disbelief and start the van. But as he drove off down the road to a restaurant for lunch, he whistled *"I'm in love, I'm in love . . ."* Glancing over at Gina, he saw that she was blushing. He almost sang the words to the song but then decided to wait. After all, tomorrow, he intended to propose.

When they returned to Stewart's Falls and Gina's home, Andy asked, "Could you help me tomorrow out at the lake? I have a lot of stuff to transfer."

When Gina agreed, Andy added, "I'll bring the food. Wear your hikers. I know a great place for a picnic. A special place. You'll like it."

* * *

Sunday turned out to be absolutely glorious. Not only was the sky cloudless, the temperature was unbelievably warm. Barely a trace of wind touched the surface of the lake. The sounds of ducks floated across the water while, in the distance, the lonely call of the loon echoed.

Gina stopped, a box of clothes in her hands, and breathed the air in. It was redolent with the earthy smells of spring. Before she reached the house, Andy came out and took the box from her. "That's the last box," she said as he headed back inside.

Something was up. Andy had literally raced up and down the stairs of his house, depositing boxes wherever they belonged. They hadn't been here fifteen minutes, and they were already finished.

Andy stepped outside, locked the door, hurried down the steps and headed for the van. Collecting his knapsack, he locked the van and then turned to Gina. Holding out his hand, he said, "Come on. The weather is perfect for my special place."

Together they headed into the forest following the path that edged the lake, stopping once to watch the ducks bobbing for food and another time to be charmed by a family of Canada Geese rafting by like some ancient Viking vessel; a parent at each end while, in between, they counted twelve tiny goslings. When the lead parent spotted them, it twisted its head to indicate its intention to move out from shore, and the silent family followed.

They went much farther this time. The path led away from shore, around fallen trees and granite outcroppings. Finally, they reached the remains of an old road. "In the winter," Andy explained, "loggers would bring out the wood. The road actually leads down to the lake where lumberjacks would stack it to send down to Stewart's Falls once the ice was out. There used to be a mill there that processed the wood."

"The road looks as if it's still used a little bit," observed Gina.

"A local farmer has my permission to cut enough wood for himself and his family so long as there's still enough for me. He's careful, cutting only trees that must be culled to keep the forest healthy."

Finally, Andy stopped and, taking his bearings, turned to Gina, his eyes dancing with excitement. "And now for my special surprise. I hope you like it as much as I do."

Taking Gina's hand, he led her carefully into a glade just off the road. There, before her, was an area sparsely treed where sun drifted down through half-budded branches to flood the ground below. The light caught the fresh green of young plants against the light brown of matted winter grasses, leaves and earth. But most wonderful was the way sunlight touched the faces of masses of trilliums.

Gina squeezed Andy's hand with awe. "I've never seen trilliums growing in the wild. Oh, I know they're our province's emblem; I see them on all the government advertisements, but I've never seen the real thing."

Hunching down, she framed a blossom, studying the long ridges of the petals and the yellow stamens. In between each petal was a smaller green leaf and on the stem were three large leaves.

Andy touched her shoulder. "Follow me," he said, and he led her carefully around the glade to the other side where two roughly-squared blocks of granite formed a convenient place to sit. Once they were settled, Andy said, "As the trilliums age, they often turn a pale pink. There are red trilliums around called Wakerobins but I've never found any in this patch." Andy looked about him and then said, "You want to eat here?"

"I can't think of a more perfect place," Gina said. "Here, let me help you set out the food."

He surprised her by saying no. "You just sit there and enjoy the scene."

He surprised her even more when he pulled out a small, collapsible table from his knapsack and placed it carefully between them. Then, to her amazement, he pulled out what seemed to be a large white tablecloth and placed it over the top of the table. Intrigued, she watched as he set two china plates on the table and silver cutlery. By now, the table was almost completely covered. Then, he sat back and surveyed his handiwork.

But he wasn't quite finished. From the knapsack, he pulled out a tall, thin crystal vase and a red silk rose. With deliberation, he placed the vase in the center of the table and stuck the rose in it. Finally satisfied, he smiled at Gina.

Gina smiled back nervously. What was he up to?

Andy cleared his throat and then said, "I wanted today to be a perfect day." Looking up at the sky, he added, "And it is. I asked Nora to make a special lunch because it is a special occasion."

Nervous now because all kinds of impossible scenarios were racing through her imagination, Gina's voice squeaked when she said, "A special occasion?"

Standing and moving around the table, Andy took her hand and pulled her up. "A very special occasion."

Gina could feel his hand trembling as he said the words and she knew that hers were trembling too. "Gina, you must know how I feel about you. You must know that I'm in love with you. I need to know. Do you feel the same way?"

Gina couldn't contain her happiness. It seemed to start at her toes and surge right up through her body. Tears flooded her eyes. Without waiting, she threw herself into his arms, almost upsetting the table. "Of course, I love you."

They had kissed before, but this time, their kisses tried to convey all the things they still had to say to each other. Finally, they eased apart. Brushing her curls back from her face, Andy said, "Then I have another question for you. Will you marry me?"

"Oh yes," Gina said, and wound her arms around his neck. Covering his face with kisses, she cried, "Yes, yes, yes."

Andy held her closely to him and breathed in the fragrance of her hair, vowing silently never to let anything come between them.

Finally, they settled back and Andy reached into the knapsack and announced, "And now for lunch."

First he brought out a plastic container with 'appetizers' carefully written on the cover. "When I told Nora we were to have a very special lunch, she rubbed her hands together and said, 'Oh I love romance. Leave it to me.' I'm not sure what she expected was going to happen."

Reaching inside the knapsack, Andy found red napkins that matched the rose. Opening the container, he found several kinds of bite-size hors d'oeuvres. Selecting a tiny toast topped with goat cheese and red-pepper jelly, he leaned across the table and popped it into Gina's mouth. Unable to resist, Gina picked up a toast and popped it into his mouth.

There is something deliciously romantic about feeding each other, Gina thought. Nora definitely had the right idea.

The next course came out of a thermal container with instructions. Carefully, Andy served delicate rounds of pastry over which he poured a tasty sauce of chicken and mushrooms. The flavor was mouth-watering. As they ate the serving, Andy began to talk about their future. "I wondered how you would feel if we lived in your house through the week and spent our weekends out on the lake."

Gina was relieved at the suggestion as she had already started to worry about where they would live. She hadn't been sure she was ready to give up on her home. "In the summer, we could spend at lot of time at the lake," she suggested. "It wouldn't be hard to commute."

"How about children?" Andy asked. "Would you like some?"

The expression on Gina's face was all he needed to know. She glowed at the thought. "It would be wonderful for us to have a family. A boy and a girl at least."

"Would you mind waiting for a little while?" he asked. "I'd like to have some time with you alone."

Gina couldn't help but lean over and take his hand. "I'd like that too. But not too long."

When they had finished their plates, Andy said, "Let's see what Nora has put in for desert."

This time, he lifted out a thick square box that was carefully tied up with a big bow. Written on the tag was a warning. *Handle with Care.* Opening the box, Andy found a red heart-shaped box which contained six truffles. A message was sitting on top of them that said, *Chocolate is for lovers.* But there was more. Sitting side by side, just beneath the chocolate box, were two tissue-wrapped goblets and a very small bottle of champagne. There was also a note in an envelope with Andy's name on it.

Mystified, Andy read the note and then laughed. "My father is a real romantic," he said. He handed the note to Gina. She read, *"I presume that, by this time, son, you've popped the question. The champagne is to help you celebrate your very special day. Dad."*

Carefully, Gina unwrapped the goblets and Andy filled them with the bubbling liquid. Then, holding his glass up, he said, "To you, my darling. May all your dreams come true."

Gina held her glass aloft and said, "To you, my love, who has made my dreams come true."

Together they sipped their champagne and fed each other the truffles. Finally, they packed up and headed back to the house. As they approached it, Andy said, "Do you think you could get an afternoon off this week?"

Gina nodded. "I'm sure I could get Wednesday afternoon off. Frequently we have an extra person in the office that day. Why?"

"I'd like to go to Toronto to see a friend who is a goldsmith. I was hoping he could design rings for us. Okay?"

"That sounds exciting. Does he make up a design from scratch?"

"He can if you wish."

"Then do you think he could work trilliums into the design?"

Stopping to hug her, Andy said, "That's a wonderful idea. I suspect it will take a week or two. Do you mind if we keep the news to ourselves until rings are finished? I think this should be Dad and Nora's time. Of course, they will have to know, but they'll keep quiet if we ask them."

Stopping to exchange another kiss, Gina said, "That's fine with me."

The Saturday of the long weekend turned out to be perfect for the opening of a new tearoom and a wedding. The village of Stewart's Falls was bursting with cottagers picking up supplies for their newly opened cottages and tourists enjoying a browse through the village's many shops. People had shed all signs of winter and were strolling along the main street in shorts and t-shirts.

As Andy drove to Gina's to pick her up for the service he took a detour past Cindy's tearoom. He could see people sitting inside through the opened windows, and others were walking up to the entrance. He was glad for Cindy and Dan's sake that they were getting business right away. They had both worked very hard to be ready on time.

Today, he drove up in a shiny red car. Getting out of it, he straightened his suit and then patted the car. Humming with satisfaction, he headed for Gina's side door when she called him from the backyard. He hurried around the shed to where Gina stood nervously, resplendent in the most beautiful blue dress he had ever seen. She gave him a shy smile and turned so that the silk flared sweetly about her lovely legs.

Walking up to her, he said softly, "You look absolutely beautiful." He kissed her on the cheek and, holding out his arm, he said, "Come on. We don't want to be late."

Gina came to a stop when she saw the red car. "Where's your van?"

"At home."

"But whose car is this?"

"Ours?"

Holding the door open for her, he said, "Actually it's for you. You'll need to have a vehicle to get to work from the lake when we stay there. I thought you might as well have the use of it now."

Gina got in the car and looked about her. It was just the right size for someone her size. Yet, when Andy folded himself into it, there seemed to be enough room. Turning to her, he said, "So you see, there is no reason for us not to get married as soon as possible. That way we can stay out at the lake during the good weather. Maybe honeymoon out there. What do you say?"

Leaning over for the kiss he had not given her when he came to the backyard, she said, "The sooner, the better."

The marriage of Jim Thompson and Nora Philips went off without a hitch. Because only family and the very closest friends of the bride and groom attended, the reception had an informality that larger affairs lacked.

Out at The Pines, Gina found herself floating about in a cloud of happiness. Andy never left her side, always within touch, a hand on her back or about her waist or her shoulder. Carolyn whispered, "You have to be the most beautiful woman here, Gina. That dress is absolutely inspired." Gina smiled and thanked her. She knew that wasn't true. Everyone at the reception seemed beautiful, but it was nice of Carolyn to say so.

After the meal had been eaten and the toasts made, Jim Thompson said, "Andy promised to sing for us before we start the dancing."

Gina looked at Andy with surprise. He'd said nothing about singing. He hadn't had his guitar in the car. However, no sooner had Jim made his request than Carolyn's husband, David, walked in the room with Andy's instrument.

Everyone settled in to listen as the evening sunlight flooded across the lake, lighting the opposite side. Slowly, its beams disappeared, leaving a lovely afterglow as Andy tuned his guitar.

At first, Andy sang songs for the bride and groom. *Plaisir d'amour* and *My love is like a red, red rose*. He sang several requests from the audience. Finally, he held up his hand and said, "I would like to finish with a new song."

Settling back in his chair, the instrument across his lap, he looked at Gina and smiled. But the first notes he played were ones of sadness and then he began to sing.

> *"The leaves had dried a rustling brown,*
> *"The grasses bleached and brittle.*
> *"A cold wind blustered all around,*
> *"The corners of my heart."*

> *"Winter had won. No love was there.*
> *"No warming winds or melting snows.*
> *"Birds found no food, the ground was bare,*
> *"In the winter of my heart."*

The music was so sad and the words so bleak that Gina found herself fighting tears as she felt his pain. But then the key changed and the chords he played lifted her spirits.

> *"And then spring came and love returned.*
> *"Green grasses blew a warm refrain.*
> *"Crocus flourished and trilliums bloomed*
> *"Ending the winter in my heart."*

At the mention of trilliums, Gina smiled at Andy, understanding exactly what his song was saying.

> *"And now, dear heart, you've changed my life,*
> *"Brought love to warm my heart's cold core,*
> *"Promised quite soon to be my wife,*
> *"Love fills the corners of my heart."*

Then, in case anyone listening had any doubt, Andy put down his guitar and walked over to Gina. Holding out his hand, he took hers and urged her to her feet. "To all those who haven't already figured it out, let me announce that Gina has agreed to be my wife." Then before their news could take over the festivities, he said to his father, "Don't you think it's time you started the dancing?"

The DJ was ready and, moments later, Nora and Jim were drifting around in each other's arms to the strains of the music. Instead of dancing, Andy said to Gina, "Come outside. I have something to show you."

Together they went outside to stand under the pines overlooking the lake. The moon was rising and a gentle breeze spread its reflection in showers of diamonds across the water. Andy drew Gina over so that the light from a window made it bright enough to see what he had in his hand.

"I picked up your ring last night. I hope you like it." Opening a velvet case, he took out the ring and, taking her hand, slipped it onto her third finger. "What do you think?"

In the light from the window, Gina studied it. It was the most beautiful ring she had ever seen. "It's got a trillium, Andy," she whispered. "Look how he's made them." Three diamond baguettes formed the white petals of the flower while three small emeralds formed the green sepals. "It's exquisite."

Tears filled her eyes as she looked at Andy and whispered, "I promise to fill your heart with love, every day of our lives together."

Crushing her to him, literally taking her breath away, he spun her around, making her laugh. "And I promise to love you," he said, "for as long as we have together, to build a home with you, to share our joys and sorrows."